A BICYCLE OF CATHAY

A Novel

I054:046

FRANK R. STOCKTON

A Bicycle of Cathay

Frank R. Stockton

© 1st World Library, 2007
PO Box 2211
Fairfield, IA 52556
www.1stworldlibrary.com
First Edition

LCCN: 2007901784

Softcover ISBN: 978-1-4218-4252-3
Hardcover ISBN: 978-1-4218-4154-0
eBook ISBN: 978-1-4218-4350-6

Purchase *"A Bicycle of Cathay"*
as a traditional bound book at:
www.1stWorldLibrary.com/purchase.asp?ISBN=978-1-4218-4252-3

1st World Library is a literary, educational organization
dedicated to:

- Creating a free internet library of downloadable ebooks

- Hosting writing competitions and offering book publishing
  scholarships.

Interested in more 1st World Library books? contact:
literacy@1stworldlibrary.com
Check us out at: www.1stworldlibrary.com

1ˢᵗ World Library Literary Society

Giving Back to the World

"If you want to work on the core problem, it's early school literacy."

- James Barksdale, former CEO of Netscape

"No skill is more crucial to the future of a child, or to a democratic and prosperous society, than literacy."

- Los Angeles Times

"Literacy... means far more than learning how to read and write... The aim is to transmit... knowledge and promote social participation."

- UNESCO

"Literacy is not a luxury, it is a right and a responsibility. If our world is to meet the challenges of the twenty-first century we must harness the energy and creativity of all our citizens."

- President Bill Clinton

"Parents should be encouraged to read to their children, and teachers should be equipped with all available techniques for teaching literacy, so the varying needs and capacities of individual kids can be taken into account."

- Hugh Mackay

CONTENTS

CHAPTER I

THE DOCTOR'S DAUGHTER

It was a beautiful summer morning when slowly I wheeled my way along the principal street of the village of Walford. A little valise was strapped in front of my bicycle; my coat, rolled into a small compass, was securely tied under the seat, and I was starting out to spend my vacation.

I was the teacher of the village school, which useful institution had been closed for the season the day before, much to the gratification of pedagogue and scholars. This position was not at all the summit of my youthful ambition. In fact, I had been very much disappointed when I found myself obliged to accept it, but when I left college my financial condition made it desirable for me to do something to support myself while engaged in some of the studies preparatory to a professional career.

I have never considered myself a sentimental person, but I must admit that I did not feel very happy that morning, and this state of mind was occasioned entirely by the feeling that there was no one who seemed to be in the least sorry that I was going away. My boys were so delighted to give up their studies that they were entirely satisfied to give up their teacher, and I am sure that my vacation would have been a very long one if they had had the ordering of it. My landlady might have been pleased to have me stay, but if I had agreed to pay my board during my absence I do not doubt that my empty room would have occasioned her no pangs of regret. I had friends in the village, but as they knew it was a matter of course that I should go away during the vacation, they seemed to be perfectly reconciled to the fact.

As I passed a small house which was the abode of my laundress, my mental depression was increased by the action of her oldest son. This little fellow, probably five years of age, and the condition of whose countenance indicated that his mother's art was seldom exercised upon it, was playing on the sidewalk with his sister, somewhat younger and much dirtier.

As I passed the little chap he looked up and in a sharp, clear voice, he cried: "Good-bye! Come back soon!" These words cut into my soul. Was it possible that this little ragamuffin was the only one in that village who was sorry to see me depart and who desired my return? And the acuteness of this cut was not decreased by the remembrance that on several occasions when he had accompanied his mother to my lodging I had given him small coins.

I was beginning to move more rapidly along the little path, well worn by many rubber tires, which edged the broad roadway, when I perceived the doctor's daughter standing at the gate of her father's front yard. As I knew her very well, and she happened to be standing there and looking in my direction, I felt that it would be the proper thing for me to stop and speak to her, and so I dismounted and proceeded to roll my bicycle up to the gate.

As the doctor's daughter stood looking over the gate, her hands clasped the tops of the two central pickets.

"Good-morning," said she. "I suppose, from your carrying

Frank R. Stockton

baggage, that you are starting off for your vacation. How far do you expect to go on your wheel, and do you travel alone?"

"My only plan," I answered, "is to ride over the hills and far away! How far I really do not know; and I shall be alone except for this good companion." And as I said this I patted the handle-bar of my bicycle.

"Your wheel does seem to be a sort of a companion," she said; "not so good as a horse, but better than nothing. I should think, travelling all by yourself in this way, you would have quite a friendly feeling for it. Did you ever think of giving it a name?"

"Oh yes," said I. "I have named it. I call it a 'Bicycle of Cathay.'"

"Is there any sense in such a name?" she asked. "It is like part of a quotation from Tennyson, isn't it? I forget the first of it."

"You are right," I said. "'Better fifty years of Europe than a cycle of Cathay.' I cannot tell you exactly why, but that seems to suggest a good name for a bicycle."

"But your machine has two wheels," said she. "Therefore you ought to say, 'Better one hundred years of Europe than two cycles of Cathay.'"

"I bow to custom," said I. "Every one speaks of a bicycle as a wheel, and I shall not introduce the plural into the name of my good steed."

"And you don't know where your Cathay is to be?" she asked.

I smiled and shook my head. "No," I answered, "but I hope

my cycle will carry me safely through it."

The doctor's daughter looked past me across the road. "I wish I were a man," said she, "and could go off as I pleased, as you do! It must be delightfully independent."

I was about to remark that too much independence is not altogether delightful, but she suddenly spoke:

"You carry very little with you for a long journey," and as she said this she grasped the pickets of the gate more tightly. I could see the contraction of the muscles of her white hands. It seemed as if she were restraining something.

"Oh, this isn't all my baggage," I replied. "I sent on a large bag to Waterton. I suppose I shall be there in a couple of days, and then I shall forward the bag to some other place."

"I do not suppose you have packed up any medicine among your other things?" she asked. "You don't look as if you very often needed medicine."

I laughed as I replied that in the course of my life I had taken but little.

"But if your cycle starts off rolling early in the morning," she said, "or keeps on late in the evening, you ought to be able to defend yourself against malaria. I do not know what sort of a country Cathay may be, but I should not be a bit surprised if you found it full of mists and morning vapors. Malaria has a fancy for strong people, you know. Just wait here a minute, please," and with that she turned and ran into the house.

I had liked the doctor's daughter ever since I had begun to know her, although at first I had found it a little hard to become acquainted with her.

Frank R. Stockton

She was the treasurer of the literary society of the village, and I was its secretary. We had to work together sometimes, and I found her a very straightforward girl in her accounts and in every other way.

In about a minute she returned, carrying a little pasteboard box.

"Here are some one-grain quinine capsules," she said. "They have no taste, and I am quite sure that if you get into a low country it would be a good thing for you to take at least one of them every morning. People may have given you all sorts of things for your journey, but I do not believe any one has given you this." And she handed me the box over the top of the gate.

I did not say that her practical little present was the only thing that anybody had given me, but I thanked her very heartily, and assured her that I would take one every time I thought I needed it. Then, as it seemed proper to do so, I straightened up my bicycle as if I would mount it. Again her fingers clutched the top of the two palings.

"When father comes home," she said, "he will be sorry to find that he had not a chance to bid you good-bye. And, by-the-way," she added, quickly, "you know there will be one more meeting of the society. Did you write out any minutes for the last evening, and would you like me to read them for you?"

"Upon my word!" I exclaimed. "I have forgotten all about it. I made some rough notes, but I have written nothing."

"Well, it doesn't matter in the least," said she, quickly. "I remember everything that happened, and I will write the minutes and read them for you; that is, if you want me to."

I assured her that nothing would please me better, and we talked a little about the minutes, after which I thought I ought not to keep her standing at the gate any longer. So I took leave of her, and we shook hands over the gate. This was the first time I had ever shaken hands with the doctor's daughter, for she was a reserved girl, and hitherto I had merely bowed to her.

As I sped away down the street and out into the open country my heart was a good deal lighter than it had been when I began my journey. It was certainly pleasant to leave that village, which had been my home for the greater part of a year, without the feeling that there was no one in it who cared for me, even to the extent of a little box of quinine capsules.

Frank R. Stockton

CHAPTER II

A BAD TWIST

It was about the middle of the afternoon that I found myself bowling along a smooth highway, bordered by trees and stretching itself almost upon a level far away into the distance. Had I been a scorcher, here would have been a chance to do a little record-breaking, for I was a powerful and practised wheelman. But I had no desire to be extravagant with my energies, and so contented myself with rolling steadily on at a speed moderate enough to allow me to observe the country I was passing through.

There were not many people on the road, but at some distance ahead of me I saw a woman on a wheel. She was not going rapidly, and I was gaining on her. Suddenly, with no reason whatever that I could see, her machine gave a twist, and, although she put out her foot to save herself, she fell to the ground. Instantly I pushed forward to assist her, but before I could reach her she was on her feet. She made a step towards her bicycle, which lay in the middle of the road, and then she stopped and stood still. I saw that she was hurt, but I could not help a sort of inward smile. "It is the old way of the world," I thought. "Would the Fates have made that young woman fall from her bicycle if there had been two men coming along on their wheels?"

As I jumped from my machine and approached her she turned her head and looked at me. She was a pale girl, and her face was troubled. When I asked her if she had hurt herself, she spoke to me without the slightest embarrassment or hesitation.

"I twisted my foot in some way," she said, "and I do not know what I am going to do. It hurts me to make a step, and I am sure I cannot work my wheel."

"Have you far to go?" I asked.

"I live about two miles from here," she answered. "I do not think I have sprained my ankle, but it hurts. Perhaps, however, if I rest for a little while I may be able to walk."

"I would not try to do that," said I. "Whatever has happened to your foot or ankle, you would certainly make it very much worse by walking such a distance. Perhaps I can ride on and get you a conveyance?"

"You would have to go a long way to get one," she answered. "We do not keep a horse and I really-"

"Don't trouble yourself in the least," I said. "I can take you to your home without any difficulty whatever. If you will mount your machine I can push you along very easily."

"But then you would have to walk yourself," she said, quickly, "and push your wheel too."

Of course it would not have been necessary for me to walk, for I could have ridden my bicycle and have pushed her along on her own, but under the circumstances I did not think it wise to risk this. So I accepted her suggestion of walking as if nothing else could be done.

Frank R. Stockton

"Oh, I do not mind walking a bit," said I. "I am used to it, and as I have been riding for a long time, it would be a relief to me."

She stood perfectly still, apparently afraid to move lest she should hurt her foot, but she raised her head and fixed a pair of very large blue eyes upon me. "It is too kind in you to offer to do this! But I do not see what else is to be done. But who is going to hold up my wheel while you help me to get on it?"

"Oh, I will attend to all that," said I, and picking up her bicycle, I brought it to her. She made a little step towards it, and then stopped.

"You mustn't do that," said I. "I will put you on." And holding her bicycle upright with my left hand, I put my right arm around her and lifted her to the seat. She was such a childlike, sensible young person that I did not think it necessary to ask any permission for this action, nor even to allude to its necessity.

"Now you might guide yourself with the handle-bar," I said. "Please steer over to that tree where I have left my machine." I easily pushed her over to the tree, and when I had laid hold of my bicycle with my left hand, we slowly proceeded along the smooth road.

"I think you would better take your feet from the pedals," said I, "and put them on the coasters - the motion must hurt you. It is better to have your injured foot raised, anyway, as that will keep the blood from running down into it and giving you more pain."

She instantly adopted my suggestion, and presently said, "That is a great deal more pleasant, and I am sure it is better for my foot to keep it still. I do hope I haven't sprained my ankle! It is possible to give a foot a bad twist without spraining it, isn't it?"

I assented, and as I did so I thought it would not be difficult to give a bad twist to any part of this slenderly framed young creature.

"How did you happen to fall?" I asked - not that I needed to inquire, for my own knowledge of wheelcraft assured me that she had tumbled simply because she did not know how to ride.

"I haven't the slightest idea," she answered. "The first thing I knew I was going over, and I wish I had not tried to save myself. It would have been better to go down bodily."

As we went on she told me that she had not had much practice, as it had been but a few weeks since she had become the possessor of a wheel, and that this was the first trip she had ever taken by herself. She had always gone in company with some one, but to-day she had thought she was able to take care of herself, like other girls. Finding her so entirely free from conventional embarrassment, I made bold to give her a little advice on the subject of wheeling in general, and she seemed entirely willing to be instructed. In fact, as I went on with my little discourse I began to think that I would much rather teach girls than boys. At first sight the young person under my charge might have been taken for a school-girl, but her conversation would have soon removed that illusion.

We had not proceeded more than a mile when suddenly I felt a very gentle tap on the end of my nose, and at the same moment the young lady turned her head towards me and exclaimed: "It's going to rain! I felt a drop!"

"I will walk faster," I said, "and no doubt I will get you to

Frank R. Stockton

your house before the shower is upon us. At any rate, I hope you won't be much wet."

"Oh, it doesn't matter about me in the least," she said. "I shall be at home and can put on dry clothes, but you will be soaked through and have to go on. You haven't any coat on!"

If I had known there was any probability of rain I should have put on my coat before I started out on this somewhat unusual method of travelling, but there was no help for it now, and all I could do was to hurry on. From walking fast I began to trot. The drops were coming down quite frequently.

"Won't that tire you dreadfully?" she said.

"Not at all," I replied. "I could run like this for a long distance."

She looked up at me with a little smile. I think she must have forgotten the pain in her foot.

"It must be nice to be strong like that," she said.

Now the rain came down faster, and my companion declared that I ought to stop and put on my coat. I agreed to this, and when I came to a suitable tree by the road-side, I carefully leaned her against it and detached my coat from my bicycle. But just as I was about to put it on I glanced at the young girl. She had on a thin shirt-waist, and I could see that the shoulders of it were already wet. I advanced towards her, holding out my coat. "I must lay this over you," I said. "I am afraid now that I shall not get you to your home before it begins to rain hard."

She turned to me so suddenly that I made ready to catch her if her unguarded movement should overturn her machine. "You mustn't do that at all!" she said. "It doesn't matter whether I am wet or not. I do not have to travel in wet clothes, and you do. Please put on your coat and let us hurry!"

I obeyed her, and away we went again, the rain now coming down hard and fast. For some minutes she did not say anything; but I did not wonder at this, for circumstances were not favorable to conversation. But presently, in spite of the rain and our haste, she spoke:

"It must seem dreadfully ungrateful and hard-hearted in me to say to you, after all you have done for me, that you must go on in the rain. Anybody would think that I ought to ask you to come into our house and wait until the storm is over. But, really, I do not see how I can do it."

I urged her not for a moment to think of me. I was hardy, and did not mind rain, and when I was mounted upon my wheel the exercise would keep me warm enough until I reached a place of shelter.

"I do not like it," she said. "It is cruel and inhuman, and nothing you can say will make it any better. But the fact is that I find myself in a very - Well, I do not know what to say about it. You are the school-teacher at Walford, are you not?"

This question surprised me, and I assented quickly, wondering what would come next.

"I thought so," she said. "I have seen you on the road on your wheel, and some one told me who you were. And now, since you have been so kind to me, I am going to tell you exactly why I cannot ask you to stop at our house. Everything is all wrong there to-day, and if I don't explain what has happened, you might think that things are worse than they really are, and I wouldn't want anybody to think that."

I listened with great attention, for I saw that she was anxious to free herself of the imputation of being inhospitable, and although the heavy rain and my rapid pace made it sometimes difficult to catch her words, I lost very little of her story.

"You see," said she, "my father is very fond of gardening, and he takes great pride in his vegetables, especially the early ones. He has peas this year ahead of everybody else in the neighborhood, and it was only day before yesterday that he took me out to look at them. He has been watching them ever since they first came up out of the ground, and when he showed me the nice big pods and told me they would be ready to pick in a day or two, he looked so proud and happy that you might have thought his peas were little living people. I truly believe that even at prayer-time he could not help thinking how good those peas would taste.

"But this morning when he came in from the garden and told mother that he was going to pick our first peas, so as to have them perfectly fresh for dinner, she said that he would better not pick them to-day, because the vegetable man had been along just after breakfast, and he had had such nice green peas that she had bought some, and therefore he had better keep his peas for some other day.

"Now, I don't want you to think that mother isn't just as good as gold, for she is. But she doesn't take such interest in garden things as father does, and to her all peas are peas, provided they are good ones. But when father heard what she had done I know that he felt exactly as if he had been stabbed in one of his tenderest places. He did not say one word, and he walked right out of the house, and since that they haven't spoken to each other. It was dreadful to sit at dinner, neither of them saying a word to the other, and only speaking to me. It was all so different from the way things generally are that I can scarcely bear it.

"And I went out this afternoon for no other reason than to give them a chance to make it up between them. I thought perhaps they would do it better if they were alone with each other. But of course I do not know what has happened, and things may be worse than they were. I could not take a stranger into the house at such a time - they would not like to be found not speaking to each other - and, besides, I do not know - "

Here I interrupted her, and begged her not to give another thought to the subject. I wanted very much to go on, and in every way it was the best thing I could do.

As I finished speaking she pointed out a pretty house standing back from the road, and told me that was where she lived. In a very few minutes after that I had run her up to the steps of her piazza and was assisting her to dismount from her wheel.

"It is awful!" she said. "This rain is coming down like a cataract!"

"You must hurry in-doors," I answered. "Let me help you up the steps." And with this I took hold of her under the arms, and in a second I had set her down in front of the closed front door. I then ran down and brought up her wheel. "Do you think you can manage to walk in?" said I.

"Oh yes!" she said. "If I can't do anything else, I can hop. My mother will soon have me all right. She knows all about such things."

She looked at me with an anxious expression, and then said, "How do you think it would do for you to wait on the piazza until the rain is over?"

"Good-bye," I said, with a laugh, and bounding down to the

front gate, where I had left my bicycle, I mounted and rode away.

The rain came down harder and harder. The road was full of little running streams, and liquid mud flew from under my whirling wheels. It was not late in the afternoon, but it was actually getting dark, and I seemed to be the only living creature out in this tremendous storm. I looked from side to side for some place into which I could run for shelter, but here the road ran between broad open fields. My coat had ceased to protect me, and I could feel the water upon my skin.

But in spite of my discomforts and violent exertions I found myself under the influence of some very pleasurable emotions, occasioned by the incident of the slender girl. Her childlike frankness was charming to me. There was not another girl in a thousand who would have told me that story of the peas. I felt glad that she had known who I was when she was talking to me, and that her simple confidences had been given to me personally, and not to an entire stranger who had happened along. I wondered if she resembled her father or her mother, and I had no doubt that to possess such a daughter they must both be excellent people.

CHAPTER III

THE DUKE'S DRESSING-GOWN

Thinking thus, I almost forgot the storm, but coming to a slight descent where the road was very smooth I became conscious that my wheel was inclined to slip, and if I were not careful I might come to grief. But no sooner had I reached the bottom of the declivity than I beheld on my right a lighted doorway. Without the slightest hesitation I turned through the wide gateway, the posts of which I could scarcely see, and stopped in front of a small house by the side of a driveway. Waiting for no permission, I carried my bicycle into a little covered porch. I then approached the door, for I was now seeking not only shelter but an opportunity to dry myself. I do not believe a sponge could have been more thoroughly soaked than I was.

At the very entrance I was met by a little man in short jacket and top-boots.

"I heard your step," said he. "Been caught in the rain, eh? Well, this is a storm! And now what're we going to do? You must come in. But you're in a pretty mess, I must say! Hi, Maria!"

At these words a large, fresh-looking woman came into the little hall.

"Maria," said the man, "here's a gentleman that's pretty nigh drowned, and he's dripping puddles big enough to swim in."

The woman smiled. "Really, sir," said she, "you've had a hard time. Wheeling, I suppose. It's an awful time to be out. It's so dark that I lighted a lamp to make things look a little cheery. But you must come in until the rain is over, and try and dry yourself."

"But how about the hall, Maria?" said the man. "There'll be a dreadful slop!"

"Oh, I'll make that all right," she said. She disappeared, and quickly returned with a couple of rugs, which she laid, wrong side up, on the polished floor of the hallway. "Now you can step on those, sir, and come into the kitchen. There's a fire there."

I thanked her, and presently found myself before a large stove, on which it was evident, from the odors, that supper was preparing. In a certain way the heat was grateful, but in less than a minute I was bound to admit to myself that I felt as if I were enveloped in a vast warm poultice. The little man and his wife - if wife she were, for she looked big enough to be his mother, and young enough to be his daughter - stood talking in the hall, and I could hear every word they said.

"It's of no use for him to try to dry himself," she said, "for he's wet to the bone. He must change his clothes, and hang those he's got on before the fire."

"Change his clothes!" exclaimed the man. "How ever can he do that? I've nothing that'll fit him, and of course he has brought nothing along with him."

"Never you mind," said she. "Something's got to be got. Take him into the little chamber. And don't consider the floor; that can be wiped up."

She came into the kitchen and spoke to me. "You must come and change your clothes," she said. "You'll catch your death of cold, else. You're the school-master from Walford, I think, sir? Indeed, I'm sure of it, for I've seen you on your wheel."

Smiling at the idea that through the instrumentality of my bicycle I had been making myself known to the people of the surrounding country, I followed the man into a small bed-chamber on the ground-floor.

"Now," said he, "the quicker you get off your wet clothes and give yourself a good rub-down the better it will be for you. And I'll go and see what I can do in the way of something for you to put on."

I asked him to bring me the bag from my bicycle, and after doing so he left me.

Very soon I heard talking outside of my door, and as both my entertainers had clear, high voices, I could hear distinctly what they said.

"Go get him the corduroys," said she. "He's a well-made man, but he's no bigger than your father was."

"The corduroys?" he said, somewhat doubtfully, I thought.

"Yes," she replied. "Go get them! I should be glad to have them put to some use."

"But what for a coat?" said he. "There's nothing in the house that he could get on."

"That's true," said she. "But he must have something. You can get him the Duke's dressing-gown."

"What!" exclaimed the man. "You don't mean - "

"Yes, I do mean," said she. "It's big enough for anybody, and it'll keep him from ketching cold. Go fetch it!"

In a short time there was a knock at my door, and the little man handed me in a pair of yellow corduroy trousers and a large and gaudy dressing-gown. "There!" said he. "They'll keep you warm until your own clothes dry."

With a change of linen from my bag, which had fortunately kept its contents dry, the yellow trousers, and a wonderful dressing-gown, made of some blue stuff embroidered with gold and lined throughout with crimson satin, I made a truly gorgeous appearance. But it struck me that it would be rather startling to a beholder were I to appear barefooted in such raiment, for my shoes and stockings were as wet as the rest of my clothes. I had not finished dressing before the little man knocked again, this time with some gray socks and a pair of embroidered slippers.

"These'll fit you, I think," said he, "for I'll lay you ten shillings that I'm as big in the feet as you are."

I would have been glad to gaze at myself in a full-length mirror, but there was no opportunity for the indulgence of such vanity; and before leaving the room I sat down for a moment to give a few thoughts to the situation. My mind first reverted to the soaked condition of my garments and the difficulty of getting them dry enough for me to put them on and continue my journey. Then I found that I had dropped the subject and was thinking of the slender girl, wondering if she had really hurt herself very much, congratulating myself that I had been fortunate enough to be on hand to help her in her need, and considering what a plight she would have been in if she had been caught in that terrible rain and utterly unable to get herself to shelter.

Suddenly I stopped short in my thinking, and going to my bag I took from it the little box of quinine capsules which had been given to me by the doctor's daughter, and promptly proceeded to swallow one of them.

"It may be of service to me," I said to myself.

When I made my appearance in the hallway I met the little man, who immediately burst into a roar of laughter.

"Lord, sir!" said he. "You must excuse me, but you look like a king on a lark! Walk into the parlor, sir, and sit down and make yourself comfortable. She's hurrying up supper to give you something warm after your wettin'. Would you like a little nip of whiskey, sir, to keep the damp out?"

I declined the whiskey, and seated myself in the neatly-furnished parlor. It was wonderful, I thought, to fall into such a hospitable household, and then I began to ask myself whether or not it would be the proper thing to offer to pay for my entertainment. I thought I had quite properly divined the position in life of the little man. This small house, so hand-somely built and neatly kept, must be a lodge upon some fine country place, and the man was probably the head gardener, or something of the kind.

It was not long before my hostess came into the room, but she did not laugh at my appearance. She was a handsome woman, erect and broad, with a free and powerful step. She smiled as she spoke to me.

"You may think that that's an over-handsome gown for such as us to be owning. It was given to my man by the Duke of Radford. That was before we were married, and he was an undergardener then. The Duchess wouldn't let the Duke wear it, because it was so gay, and there wasn't none of the servants that would care to take it, for fear they'd be laughed

Frank R. Stockton

at, until they offered it to John. And John, you must know, he'd take anything! But I came in to tell you supper's ready; and, if you like, I'll bring you something in here, and you can eat it on that table, or - "

Here I interrupted my good hostess, and declared that, while I should be glad to have some supper, I would not eat any unless I might sit down with her husband and herself; and, as this proposition seemed to please her, the three of us were soon seated around a very tastefully furnished table in a dining-room looking out upon a pretty lawn. The rain had now almost ceased, and from the window I could see beautiful stretches of grass, interspersed with ornamental trees and flower-beds.

The meal was plain but abundant, with an appetizing smell pervading it which is seldom noticed in connection with the tables of the rich. When we had finished supper I found that the skies had nearly cleared and that it was growing quite light again. I asked permission to step out upon a little piazza which opened from the dining-room and smoke a pipe, and while I was sitting there enjoying the beauty of the sunlight on the sparkling grass and trees I again heard the little man and his wife talking to each other.

"It can't be done," said he, speaking very positively. "I've orders about that, and there's no getting round them."

"It's got to be done!" said she, "and there's an end of it! The clothes won't be dry until morning, and it won't do to put them too near the stove, or they'll shrink so he can't get them on. And he can't go away to hunt up lodgings wearing the Duke's dressing-gown and them yellow breeches!"

"Orders is orders," said the man, "and unless I get special leave, it can't be done."

"Well, then, go and get special leave," said she, "and don't stand there talking about it!"

There was no doubt that my lodging that night was the subject of this conversation, but I had no desire to interfere with the good intentions of my hostess. I must stay somewhere until my clothes were dry, and I should be glad to stop in my present comfortable quarters.

So I sat still and smoked, and very soon I heard the big shoes of the little man grating upon the gravel as he walked rapidly away from the house. Now came the good woman out upon the piazza to ask me if I had found my tobacco dry. "Because if it's damp," said she, "my man has some very good 'baccy in his jar."

I assured her that my pouch had kept dry; and then, as she seemed inclined to talk, I begged her to sit down if she did not mind the pipe. Down she sat, and steadily she talked. She congratulated herself on her happy thought to light the hall lamp, or I might never have noticed the house in the darkness, and she would have been sorry enough if I had had to keep on the road for another half-hour in that dreadful rain.

On she talked in the most cheerful and communicative way, until suddenly she rose with a start. "He's coming himself, sir!" she said, "with Miss Putney."

"Who is 'he'?" I asked.

"It's the master, sir Mr. Putney, and his daughter. Just stay here where you are, sir, and make yourself comfortable. I'll go and speak to them."

Left to myself, I knocked out my pipe and sat wondering what would happen next. A thing happened which surprised

Frank R. Stockton

me very much. Upon a path which ran in front of the little piazza there appeared two persons - one, an elderly gentleman, with gray side-whiskers and a pale face, attired in clothes with such an appearance of newness that it might well have been supposed this was the first time he had worn them; the other, a young lady, rather small in stature, but extremely pleasant to look upon. She had dark hair and large blue eyes; her complexion was rich, and her dress of light silk was wonderfully well shaped.

All this I saw at a glance, and immediately afterwards I also perceived that she had most beautiful teeth; for when she beheld me as I rose from my chair and stood in my elevated position before her she could not restrain a laugh; but for this apparent impoliteness I did not blame her at all.

But not so much as a smile came upon the countenance of the elderly gentleman. He, too, was small, but he had a deep voice. "Good-evening, sir," said he. "I am told that you are the school-master at Walford, and that you were overtaken by the storm."

I assured him that these were the facts, and stood waiting to hear what he would say next.

"It was very proper indeed, sir, that my gardener and his wife should take you under the protection of this roof, but as I hear that it is proposed that you should spend the night here, I have come down to speak about it. I will tell you at once, sir, that I have given my man the most positive orders that he is not to allow any one to spend a night in this house. It is so conveniently near to the road that I should not know what sort of persons were being entertained here if I allowed him any such privilege."

As he spoke the young lady stood silently gazing at me. There was a remnant of a smile upon her face, but I could also see that she was a little annoyed. I was about to make some sort of an independent answer to the gentleman's remarks, but he anticipated me.

"I do not want you to think, sir, on account of what I have said, that I intend to drive you off my property at this hour of the evening, and in your inappropriate clothing. I have heard of you, sir, and you occupy a position of trust and, to a certain degree, of honor, in your village. Therefore, while I cannot depart from my rule - for I wish to make no precedent of that kind - I will ask you to spend the night at my house. You need not be annoyed by the peculiarity of your attire. If you desire to avoid observation you can remain here until it grows darker, and then you can walk up to the mansion. I shall have a bed-room prepared for you, and whenever you choose you can occupy it. I have been informed that you have had something to eat, and it is as well, for perhaps your dress would prevent you from accepting an invitation to our evening meal."

I still held my brier-wood pipe in my hand, and I felt inclined to hurl it at the dapper head of the consequential little gentleman, but with such a girl standing by it would have been impossible to treat him with any disrespect, and as I looked at him I felt sure that his apparent superciliousness was probably the result of too much money and too little breeding.

The young lady said nothing, but she turned and looked steadily at her father. Her countenance was probably in the habit of very promptly expressing the state of her mind, and it now seemed to say to her father, "I hope that what you have said will not make him decline what you offer!"

My irritation quickly disappeared. I had now entered into my Cathay, and I must take things as I found them there. As I could not stay where I was, and could not continue my journey, it would be a sensible thing to overlook the man's manner and accept his offer, and I accordingly did so. I think he was pleased more than he cared to express.

"Very good, sir!" said he. "As soon as it grows a little darker I shall be glad to have you walk up to my house. As I said before, I am sure you would not care to do so now, as you might provoke remarks even from the servants. Good-evening, sir, until I see you again."

During all this time the young lady had not spoken, but as the two disappeared around the corner of the house I heard her voice. She spoke very clearly and distinctly, and she said, "It would have been a great deal more gracious if you had asked him to come at once, without all that - " The rest of her remarks were lost to me.

The little man and his wife presently came out on the porch. Her countenance expressed a sort of resignation to thwarted hospitality.

"It's the way of the world, sir!" she said. "The ups are always up and the downs are always down! I expect they will be glad to have company at the house, for it must be dreadfully lonely up there - which might be said of this house as well."

It soon became dark enough for me to walk through the grounds without hurting the sensibilities of their proprietor, and as I arose to go the good wife of the gardener brought me my cap.

"I dried that out for you, sir, for I knew you would want it, and to-morrow morning my man will take your clothes up to the house."

I thanked her for her thoughtful kindness, and was about to depart, but the little man was not quite ready for me to go.

"If you don't mind, sir," said he, "and would step back there in the light just for one minute, I would like to take another look at you. I don't suppose I'll ever see anybody again wearing the Duke's dressing-gown. By George, sir, you do look real royal!"

His wife looked at me admiringly. "Yes, sir," said she, "and I wish it was the fashion for gentlemen to dress something like that every day. But I will say, sir, that if you don't want people to be staring at you, and will just wrap that gown round you so that the lining won't be seen, you won't look so much out of the way."

As I walked along the smooth, hard driveway I adopted the suggestion of the gardener's wife; but as I approached the house, and saw that even the broad piazza was lighted by electric lamps, I was seized with the fancy to appear in all my glory, and I allowed my capacious robe to float out on each side of me in crimson brightness.

The gentleman stood at the top of the steps. "I have been waiting for you, sir," said he. He looked as if he were about to offer me his hand, but probably considered this an unnecessary ceremony under the circumstances. "Would you like to retire to your room, sir, or would you prefer - prefer sitting out here to enjoy the cool of the evening? Here are chairs and seats, sir, of all variety of comfort. My family and I frequently sit out here in the evenings, but to-night the air is a little damp."

I assured the gentleman that the air suited me very well, and that I would prefer not to retire so early; and so, not caring any longer to stand in front of the lighted doorway, I walked to one end of the piazza and took a seat.

"We haven't yet - that is to say, we are still at the table," he remarked, as he followed me; "but if there is anything that

Frank R. Stockton

you would like to have, I should be - "

I interrupted him by declaring that I had supped heartily and did not want for anything in the world, and then, with some sort of an inarticulate excuse, he left me. I knew very well that this nervously correct personage had jumped up from his dinner in order that he might meet me at the door and thus prevent my unconventional attire from shocking any of the servants.

It was very quiet and pleasant on the piazza, but, although I could hear that a great deal of talking was going on inside, no words came to me. In a short time, however, a man-servant in livery came out upon the piazza and approached me with a tray on which were a cup of coffee and some cigars. I could not refrain from smiling as I saw the man.

"The old fellow has been forced to conquer his prejudices," I said to myself, "and to submit to the mortification of allowing me to be seen by his butler!"

I think, however, that even had the master been regarding us he would have seen no reason for mortification in the manner of his servant. The man was extremely polite and attentive, suggesting various refreshments, such as wine and biscuits, and I never was treated by a lackey with more respect.

Leaning back in a comfortable chair, I sipped my coffee and puffed away at a perfectly delightful Havana cigar. "Cathay is not a bad place," said I, to myself. "Its hospitality is a little queer, but as to gorgeousness, luxury, and - " I was about to add another quality when my mind was diverted by a light step on the piazza, and, turning my head, I beheld the young lady I had seen before. Instantly I rose and laid aside my cigar.

"Please do not disturb yourself," she said. "I simply came out to give a little message from my father. Sit down again, and I will take this seat for a moment. My father's health is delicate," she said, "and we do not like him to be out in the night air, especially after a rain. So I came in his stead to tell you that if you would like to come into the house you must do so without the slightest hesitation, because my mother and I do not mind that dressing-gown any more than if it were an ordinary coat. We are very glad to have the opportunity of entertaining you, for we know some people in Walford - not very many, but some - and we have heard you and your school spoken of very highly. So we want you to make yourself perfectly at home, and come in or sit out here, just as your own feelings in regard to extraordinary fine clothes shall prompt you."

At this she reassured me as to the beauty of her teeth. "As long as you will sit out here," said I, to myself, "there will be no in-doors for me."

She seemed to read my thoughts, and said: "If you will go on with your smoking, I will wait and ask you some things about Walford. I dearly love the smell of a good cigar, and father never smokes. He always keeps them, however, in case of gentlemen visitors."

She then went on to talk about some Walford people, and asked me if I knew Mary Talbot. I replied in the affirmative, for Miss Talbot was a member of our literary society, and the young lady informed me that Mary Talbot had a brother in my school - a fact of which I was aware to my sorrow - and it was on account of this brother that she had first happened to see me.

"See me!" I exclaimed, with surprise.

"Yes," said she. "I drove over to the village one day this

spring, and Mary and I were walking past your school-house, and the door was wide open, for it was so warm, and we stopped so that Mary might point out her brother to me; and so, as we were looking in, of course I saw you."

"And you recognized me," I said, "when you saw me at the gardener's house?"

"We call that the lodge," said she. "Not that I care in the least what name you give it. And while we are on a personal subject, I want to ask you to excuse me for laughing at you when I first saw you in that astounding garb. It was very improper, I know, but the apparition was so sudden I could not help it."

I had never met a young lady so thoroughly self-contained as this one. None of the formalities of society had been observed in regard to our acquaintance with each other, but she talked with me with such an easy grace and with such a gentle assurance that there was no need of introduction or presentation; I felt acquainted with her on the spot. I had no doubt that her exceptionally gracious demeanor was due to the fact that nobody else in the house seemed inclined to be gracious, and she felt hospitality demanded that something of the kind should be offered me by some one of the family.

We talked together for some minutes longer, and then, apparently hearing something in the house which I did not notice, she rose rather abruptly.

"I must go in," she said; "but don't you stay out here a second longer than you want to."

She had left me but a very short time when her father came out on the piazza, his coat buttoned up nearly to his chin. "I have been detained, sir," he said, "by a man who came to see me on business. I cannot remain with you out here, for the air affects me; but if you will come in, sir, I shall be glad to have you do so, without regard to your appearance. My wife is not strong and she has retired, and if it pleases you I shall be very glad to have you tell me something of your duties and success in Walford. Or, if you are fatigued, your room is ready for you, and my man will show you to it."

I snatched at the relief held out to me. To sit in the company of that condescending prig, to bore him and to be bored by him, was a doleful grievance I did not wish to inflict upon myself, and I eagerly answered that the day had been a long and hard one, and that I would be glad to go to bed.

This was an assertion which was doubly false, for I was not in the least tired or sleepy; and just as I had made the statement and was entering the hall I saw that the young lady was standing at the parlor door; but it was too late now for me to change my mind.

"Brownster," said Mr. Putney to his butler, "will you give this gentleman a candle and show him to his room?"

Brownster quietly bowed, and stepping to a table in the corner, on which stood some brass bed-room candlesticks, he lighted one of the candles and stood waiting.

The gentleman moved towards his daughter, and then he stopped and turned to me. "We have breakfast," he said, "at half-past eight But if that is too late for you," he added, with a certain hesitation, "you can have - "

At this moment I distinctly saw his daughter punch him with her elbow, and as I had no desire to make an early start, and wished very much to enjoy a good breakfast in Cathay, I quickly declared that I was in no hurry, and that the family breakfast hour would suit me perfectly.

The young lady disappeared into the parlor, and I moved towards the butler; but my host, probably thinking that he had not been quite as attentive to me as his station demanded, or wishing to let me see what a fine house he possessed, stepped up to me and asked me to look into the billiard-room, the door of which I was about to pass. After some remarks of deprecatory ostentation, in which he informed me that in building his house he thought only of comfort and convenience, and nothing of show, he carelessly invited my attention to the drawing-room, the library, the music-room, and the little sitting-room, all of which were furnished with as much stiffness and hardness and inharmonious coloring as money could command.

When we had finished the round of these rooms he made me a bow as stiff as one of his white and gold chairs, and I followed the butler up the staircase. The man with the light preceded me into a room on the second floor, and just as I was about to enter after him I saw the young lady come around a corner of the hall with a lighted candle in her hand.

"Good-night," she said, with a smile so charming that I wanted to stop and tell her something about Mary Talbot's brother; but she passed on, and I went into my room.

It seemed perfectly ridiculous to me that people should carry around bed-room candles in a house lighted from top to bottom by electricity, but I had no doubt that this was one of the ultra-conventional customs from which the dapper gentleman would not allow his family to depart. I did not believe for a moment that his daughter would conform to such nonsense except to please her parent.

The softly moving and attentive Brownster put the candle on the table, blew it out, and touched a button, thereby lighting up a very handsomely furnished room. Then, after performing every possible service for me, with a bow he left me.

Throwing myself into a great easy chair, I kicked off my embroidered slippers and put my feet upon another chair gay with satin stripes. Raising my eyes, I saw in front of me a handsome mirror extending from the floor nearly to the ceiling, and at the magnificent personage which therein met my gaze I could not help laughing aloud.

I rose, stood before the mirror, folded my gorgeous gown around me, spread it out, contrasting the crimson glory of its lining with the golden yellow of my trousers, and wondered in my soul how that exceedingly handsome girl with the bright eyes could have controlled her risibilities as she sat with me on the piazza. I could see that she had a wonderful command of herself, but this exercise of it seemed superhuman.

I walked around the sumptuously furnished chamber, looking at the pictures and bric-a-brac; I wondered that the master of the house was willing to put me in a room like this - I had expected a hall bed-room, at the best; I sat down by an open window, for it was very early yet and I did not want to go to bed, but I had scarcely seated myself when I heard a tap at the door. I could not have explained it, but this tap made me jump, and I went to the door and opened it instead of calling out. There stood the butler, with a tray in his hand on which was a decanter of wine, biscuits, cheese, and some cigars.

"It's so early, sir," said Brownster, "that she said - I mean, sir, I thought that you might like something to eat, and if you want to enjoy a cigar before retiring, as many gentlemen do, you need not mind smoking here. These rooms are so well ventilated, sir, that every particle of odor will be out in no time." Placing the tray upon a table, he retired.

For an hour or more I sat sipping my wine, puffing smoke into rings, and allowing my mind to dwell pleasingly upon the situation, the most prominent feature of which seemed to me to be a young lady with bright eyes and white teeth, and dressed in a perfectly-fitting gown.

When at last I thought I ought to go to bed, I stood and gazed at my little valise. I had left it on the porch and had totally forgotten it, but here it was upon a table, where it had been placed, no doubt, by the thoughtful Brownster. I opened it and took out the box of capsules. I did not feel that I had taken cold in the night air; this was not a time to protect myself against morning mists; but still I thought it would be well for me to swallow a capsule, and I did so.

CHAPTER IV

A BIT OF ADVICE

The next morning I awoke about seven o'clock. My clothes, neatly brushed and folded, were on a chair near the bed, with my brightly-blackened shoes near by. I rose, quickly dressed myself, and went forth into the morning air. I met no one in the house, and the hall door was open. For an hour or more I walked about the beautiful grounds. Sometimes I wandered near the house, among the flower-beds and shrubs; sometimes I followed the winding path to a considerable distance; occasionally I sat down in a covered arbor; and then I sought the shade of a little grove, in which there were hammocks and rustic chairs. But I met no one, and I saw no one except some men working near the stables. I would have been glad to go down to the lodge and say "Good-morning" to my kind entertainers there, but for some reason or other it struck me that that neat little house was too much out of the way.

When I had had enough walking I retired to the piazza and sat there, until Brownster, with a bow, came and informed me that breakfast was served.

The young lady, in the freshest of summer costumes, met me at the door and bade me "Good-morning," but the greeting of her father was not by any means cordial, although his manner had lost some of the stiff condescension which had

Frank R. Stockton

sat so badly upon him the evening before. The mother was a very pleasant little lady of few words and a general air which indicated an intimate acquaintance with back seats.

The breakfast was a remarkably good one. When the meal was over, Mr. Putney walked with me into the hall. "I must now ask you to excuse me, sir," said he, "as this is the hour when I receive my manager and arrange with him for the varied business of the day. Good-morning, sir. I wish you a very pleasant journey." And, barely giving me a chance to thank him for his entertainment, he disappeared into the back part of the house.

The young lady was standing at the front of the hall. "Won't you please come in," she said, "and see mother? She wants to talk to you about Walford."

I found the little lady in a small room opening from the parlor, and also, to my great surprise, I found her extremely talkative and chatty. She asked me so many questions that I had little chance to answer them, and she told me a great deal more about Walford and its people and citizens than I had learned during my nine months' residence in the village. I was very glad to give her an opportunity of talking, which was a pleasure, I imagined, she did not often enjoy; but as I saw no signs of her stopping, I was obliged to rise and take leave of her.

The young lady accompanied me into the hall. "I must get my valise," I said, "and then I must be off. And I assure you - "

"No, do not trouble yourself about your valise," she interrupted. "Brownster will attend to that - he will take it down to the lodge. And as to your gorgeous raiment, he will see that that is all properly returned to its owners."

I picked up my cap, and she walked with me out upon the piazza. "I suppose you saw everything on our place," she asked, "when you were walking about this morning?"

A little surprised, I answered that I had seen a good deal, but I did not add that I had not found what I was looking for.

"We have all sorts of hot-houses and green-houses," she said, "but they are not very interesting at this time of the year, otherwise I would ask you to walk through them before you go." She then went on to tell me that a little building which she pointed out was a mushroom-house. "And you will think it strange that it should be there when I tell you that not one of our family likes mushrooms or ever tastes one. But the manager thinks that we ought to grow mushrooms, and so we do it."

As she was talking, the thought came to me that there were some people who might consider this young lady a little forward in her method of entertaining a comparative stranger, but I dismissed this idea. With such a peculiarly constituted family it was perhaps necessary for her to put herself forward, in regard, at least, to the expression of hospitality.

"One thing I must show you," she said, suddenly, "and that is the orchid-house! Are you fond of orchids?"

"Under certain circumstances," I said, unguardedly, "I could be fond of apple-cores." As soon as I had spoken these words I would have been glad to recall them, but they seemed to make no impression whatever on her.

We walked to the orchid-house, we went through it, and she explained all its beauties, its singularities, and its rarities. When we came out again, I asked myself: "Is she in the habit of doing all this to chance visitors? Would she treat a Brown or a Robinson in the way she is treating me?" I could not answer my question, but if Brown and Robinson had appeared at that moment I should have been glad to knock their heads together.

I did not want to go; I would have been glad to examine every building on the place, but I knew I must depart; and as I was beginning to express my sense of the kindness with which I had been treated, she interrupted by asking me if I expected to come back this way.

"No," said I, "that is not my plan. I expect to ride on to Waterton, and there I shall stop for a day or two and decide what section of the country I shall explore next."

"And to-day?" she said. "Where have you planned to spend the night?"

"I have been recommended to stop at a little inn called the 'Holly Sprig,'" I replied. "It is a leisurely day's journey from Walford, and I have been told that it is a pleasant place and a pretty country. I do not care to travel all the time, and I want to stop a little when I find interesting scenery."

"Oh, I know the Holly Sprig Inn," said she, speaking very quickly, "and I would advise you not to stop there. We have lunched there two or three times when we were out on long drives. There is a much better house about five miles the other side of the Holly Sprig. It is really a large, handsome hotel, with good service and everything you want - where people go to spend the summer."

I thanked her for her information and bade her good-bye. She shook my hand very cordially and I walked away. I had gone but a very few steps when I wanted to turn around and look back, but I did not.

Before I had reached the lodge, where I had left my bicycle, I met Brownster, and when I saw him I put my hand into my pocket. He had certainly been very attentive.

"I carried your valise, sir," he said, "to the lodge, and I took the liberty of strapping it to your handle-bar. You will find everything all right, sir, and the - other clothes will be properly attended to."

I thanked him, and then handed him some money. To my surprise, he did not offer to take it. He smiled a little and bowed.

"Would you mind, sir," he said, "if you did not give me anything? I assure you, sir, that I'd very much rather that you wouldn't give me anything." And with this he bowed and rapidly disappeared.

"Well," said I, to myself, as I put my money back into my pocket, "it is a queer country, this Cathay."

As I approached the lodge, I felt that perhaps I had received a lesson, but I was not sure. I would wait and let circumstances decide. The gardener was away attending to his duties; but his wife was there, and when she came forward, with a frank, cheery greeting, I instantly decided that I had had a lesson. I thanked her, as earnestly as I knew how, for what she had done for me, and then I added:

"You and your husband have treated me with such kind hospitality that I am not going to offer you anything in return for what you have done."

"You would have hurt us, sir, if you had," said she.

Then, in order to change the subject, I spoke of the honor which had been bestowed upon me by being allowed to wear the Duke's dressing-gown. She smiled, and replied:

"Honors would always be easy for you, sir, if you only chose to take them."

As I rode away I thought that the last remark of the gardener's wife seemed to show a mental brightness above her station, although I did not know exactly what she meant. "Can it be," I asked myself, "that she fancies that good family, six feet of athletic muscle, and no money would be considered sufficient to make matrimonial honors easy on that estate?" If such an idea had come into her head, it certainly was a very foolish one, and I determined to drive it from my mind by thinking of something else.

Suddenly I slackened my speed. I stopped and put one foot to the ground. What a hard-hearted wretch I thought myself to be! Here I was thinking of all sorts of nonsense and speeding away without a thought of the young girl who had hurt herself the day before and who had been helped by me to her home! She lived but a few miles back, and I had determined, the evening before, to run down and see how she was getting on before starting on my day's journey.

I turned and went bowling back over the road on which I had been so terribly drenched the previous afternoon. In a very little while my bicycle was leaning against the fence of the pretty house by the road-side, and I had entered the front yard. The slender girl was sitting on the piazza behind some vines. When she saw me she quickly closed the book she was reading, drew one foot from a little stool, and rose to meet me. There was more color on her face than I had supposed would be likely to find its way there, and her bright eyes showed that she was not only surprised but glad to see me.

"I thought you were ever so far on your journey!" she said.

"And how did you get through that awful storm?"

"I want to know first about your foot," I said - "how is that?"

"My own opinion is," she answered, "that it is nearly well. Mother knew exactly what to do for it; she wrapped it in wet cloths and dry cloths, and this morning I scarcely think of it. But there is one thing I want to tell you before you meet father and mother - for they want to see you, I know. We talked a great deal about you last night. You may have thought it strange I told you about the peas, but I had to do it to explain why I could not ask you to stop. Now I want to tell you that this accident made everything all right. As soon as father and mother knew that I was hurt they forgot everything else, and neither of them remembered that there was such a thing as a pea-vine in the world. It really seems as if my tumble was a most lucky thing. And now you must come in. They will never forgive me if I let you go away without seeing them."

The mother, a pleasant little woman, full of cheerful gratitude to me for having done so much for her daughter, and the father, tall and slender, hurrying in from the garden, his face beaming with a friendly enthusiasm, apologizing for the mud on his clothes, and almost in the same breath telling me of the obligations under which I had placed him, both seemed to me at the first glance to be such kind, simple-hearted, simple-mannered people that I could not help contrasting this family with the one under whose roof I had passed the night.

I spent half an hour with these good people, patiently listening to their gratitude and to their deep regrets that I had been allowed to go on in the storm; but I succeeded in allaying their friendly regrets by assuring them that it would have been impossible to keep me from going on, so certain had I been that I could reach the little town of Vernon before the storm grew violent. Then I was obliged to tell them that I did not reach Vernon, and how I had spent the night.

"With the Putneys!" exclaimed the mother. "I am sure you could not have been entertained in a finer house!"

They asked me many questions and I told them many things, and I soon discovered that they took a generous interest in the lives of other people. They spoke of the good this rich family had done in the neighborhood during the building of their great house and the improvement of their estate, and not a word did I hear of ridicule or scandalous comment, although in good truth there was opportunity enough for it.

The young lady asked me if I had seen Miss Putney, and when I replied that I had, she inquired if I did not think that she was a very pretty girl. "I do not know her," she said, "but I have often seen her when she was out driving. I do not believe there is any one in this part of the country who dresses better than she does."

I laughed, and told her that I thought I knew somebody who dressed much finer even than Miss Putney, and then I described the incident of the Duke's dressing-gown. This delighted them all, and before I left I was obliged to give every detail of my gorgeous attire.

It was about eleven o'clock when at last I tore myself away from this most attractive little family. To live as they lived, to be interested in the things that interested them - for the house seemed filled with books and pictures - to love nature, to love each other, and to think well of their fellow-beings, even of the super-rich - seemed to me to be an object for which a man of my temperament should be willing to strive and thankful to win. After meeting her parents I did not wonder that I had thought the slender girl so honest-hearted and so lovable. It was true that I had thought that.

CHAPTER V

THE LADY AND THE CAVALIER

The day was fine, and the landscape lay clean and sharply defined under the blue sky and white clouds. I sped along in a cheerful mood, well pleased with what my good cycle had so far done for me. Again I passed the open gate of the Putney estate, and glanced through it at the lodge. I saw no one, and was glad of it - better pleased, perhaps, than I could have given good reason for. When I had gone on a few hundred yards I was suddenly startled by a voice - a female voice.

"Well! well!" cried some one on my right, and turning, I saw, above a low wall, the head and shoulders of the young lady with the dark eyes with whom I had parted an hour or so before. A broad hat shaded her face, her eyes were very dark and very wide open, and I saw some of her beautiful teeth, although she was not smiling or laughing. It was plain that she had not come down there to see me pass; she was genuinely astonished; I dismounted and approached the wall.

"I thought you were miles and miles on your way!" said she. It occurred to me that I had recently heard a remark very like this, and yet the words, as they came from the slender girl and from this one, seemed to have entirely different meanings. She was desirous, earnestly desirous, to know how I came to be passing this place at this time, when I had left their gate so long before, and, as I was not unwilling to gratify her curiosity, I told her the whole story of the accident the day before, and of everything which had followed it.

"And you went all the way back," she said, "to inquire after that Burton girl?"

"Do you know her?" I asked.

"No," she said, "I do not know her; but I have seen her often, and I know all about her family. They seem to be of such little consequence, one way or the other, that I can scarcely understand how things could so twist themselves that you should consider it necessary to go back there this morning before you really started on your day's journey."

I do not remember what I said, but it was something commonplace, no doubt, but I imagined I perceived a little pique in the young lady. Of course I did not object to this, for nothing could be more flattering to a young man than the exhibition of such a feeling on an occasion such as this.

But if she felt any pique she quickly brushed it out of sight, for, as I have said before, she was a young woman who had great command of herself. Of course I said to her that I was very glad to have this chance of seeing her again, and she answered, with a laugh:

"If you really are glad, you ought to thank the Burton girl. This is one of my favorite walks. The path runs along inside the wall for a considerable distance and then turns around the little hill over there, and so leads back to the house. When I happened to look over the wall and saw you I was truly surprised."

The ground was lower on the outside of the wall than on the inside, and as I stood and looked almost into the eyes of this girl, as she leaned with her arms upon the smooth top of the wall, the idea which the gardener's wife put into my head came into it again. This was a beautiful face, and the expression upon it was different from anything I had seen there before. Her surprise had disappeared, her pique had gone, but a very great interest in the incident of my passing this spot at the moment of her being there was plainly evident. As I gazed at her my blood ran warmer through my veins, and there came upon me a feeling of the olden time - of the days when the brave cavalier rode up to the spot where, waiting for him, his lady sat upon her impatient jennet.

Without the least hesitation, I asked:

"Do you ride a wheel?"

She looked wonderingly at me for a moment, and then broke into a laugh.

"Why on earth do you ask such a question as that? I have a bicycle, but I am not a very good rider, and I never venture out upon the public road by myself."

"You shouldn't think of such a thing," said I; and then I stood silent, and my mind showed me two young people, each mounted, not upon a swift steed, but upon a far swifter pair of wheels, skimming onward through the summer air, still rolling on, on, on, through country lanes and woodland roads, laughing at pursuit if they heard the trampling of eager hoofs behind them, with never a telegraph wire to stretch menacingly above them, and so on, on, on, their eyes sparkling, their hearts beating high with youthful hope.

Again, through the tender mists of the afternoon, I saw them returning from some secluded Gretna Green to bend their knees and bow their heads before the lord of the fair bride's home.

When all this had passed through my brain, I wondered how such a pair would be received. I knew the gardener and his wife would welcome them, to begin with; Brownster would be very glad to see them; and I believe the mother would stand with tears of joy and open arms, in whatever quiet room she might feel free to await them. Moreover, when the sterner parent heard my tale and read my pedigree, might he not consider good name on the one side an equivalent for good money on the other?

I looked up at her; she did not ask me what I had been thinking about nor remark upon my silence. She, too, had been wrapped in revery; her face was grave. She raised her arms from the wall and stood up.

It was plainly time for me to do something, and she decided the point for me by slightly moving away from the wall. "Some time, when you are riding out from Walford," she said, "we should be glad to have you stop and take luncheon. Father likes to have people at luncheon."

"I should be delighted to do so," said I; and if she had asked me to delay my journey and take luncheon with them that day I think I should have accepted the invitation. But she did not do that, and she was not a young lady who would stand too long by a public road talking to a young man. She smiled very sweetly and held out her hand over the wall. "Good-bye again," she said. As I took her hand I felt very much inclined to press it warmly, but I refrained. Her grasp was firm and friendly, and I would have liked very much to know whether or not it was more so than was her custom.

I was mounting my wheel when she called to me again.

"Now, I suppose," she said, "you are going straight on?"

"Oh yes," I replied, with emphasis, "straight on."

"And the name of the hotel where you will stay to-night," said she, "it is the Cheltenham. I forgot it when I spoke to you before. I do not believe, really, it is more than three miles beyond the other little place where you thought of stopping."

Then she walked away from the wall and I mounted. I moved very slowly onward, and as I turned my head I saw that a row of straggling bushes which grew close to the wall were now between her and me. But I also saw, or thought I saw, between the leaves and boughs, that her face was towards me, and that she was waving her handkerchief. If I had been sure of that, I think I should have jumped over the wall, pushed through the bushes, and should have asked her to give me that handkerchief, that I might fasten it on the front of my cap as, in olden days, a knight going forth to his adventures bound upon his helmet the glove of his lady-love.

But I was not sure of it, and, seized by a sudden energetic excitement, I started off at a tremendous rate of speed. The ground flew backward beneath me as if I had been standing on the platform of a railroad car. Not far ahead of me there came from a side road into the main avenue on which I was travelling a Scorcher, scorching. As he spun away in front of me, his body bent forward until his back was nearly horizontal, and his green-stockinged legs striking out behind him with the furious rapidity of a great frog trying to push his head into the mud, he turned back his little face with a leer of triumphant derision at every moving thing which might happen to be behind him.

At the sight of this green-legged Scorcher my blood rose, and it was with me as if I had heard the clang of trumpets

Frank R. Stockton

and the clash of arms. I leaned slightly forward; I struck out powerfully, swiftly, and steadily; I gained upon the Scorcher; I sent into his emerald legs a thrill of startled fear, as if he had been a terrified hare bounding madly away from a pursuing foe, and I passed him as if I had been a swift falcon swooping by a quarry unworthy of his talons.

On, on I sped, not deigning even to look back. The same spirit possessed me as that which fired the hearts of the olden knights. I would have been glad to meet with another Scorcher, and yet another, that for the sake of my fair lady I might engage with each and humble his pride in the dust.

"It is true," I said to myself, with an inward laugh, "I carry no glove or delicate handkerchief bound upon my visor - " but at this point my mind wandered. I went more slowly, and at last I stopped and sat down under the shade of a way-side tree. I thought for a few minutes, and then I said to myself, "It seems to me this would be a good time to take one of those capsules," and I took one. I then fancied that perhaps I ought to take two, but I contented myself with one.

CHAPTER VI

THE HOLLY SPRIG INN

In the middle of the day I stopped at Vernon, and the afternoon was well advanced when I came in sight of a little way-side house with a broad unfenced green in front of it, and a swinging sign which told the traveller that this was the "Holly Sprig Inn."

I dismounted on the opposite side of the road and gazed upon the smoothly shaven greensward in front of the little inn; upon the pretty upper windows peeping out from their frames of leaves; upon the queerly-shaped projections of the building; upon the low portico which shaded the doorway; and upon the gentle stream of blue smoke which rose from the great gray chimney.

Then I turned and looked over the surrounding country. There were broad meadows slightly descending to a long line of trees, between which I could see the glimmering of water. On the other side of the road, and extending back of the inn, there were low, forest-crowned hills. Then my eyes, returning to nearer objects, fell upon an old-fashioned garden, with bright flowers and rows of box, which lay beyond the house.

"Why on earth," I thought, "should I pass such a place as this

Frank R. Stockton

and go on to the Cheltenham, with its waiters in coat tails, its nurse-maids, and its rows of people on piazzas? She could not know my tastes, and perhaps she had thought but little on the subject, and had taken her ideas from her father. He is just the man to be contented with nothing else than a vast sprawling hotel, with disdainful menials expecting tips."

I rolled my bicycle along the little path which ran around the green, and knocked upon the open door of Holly Sprig Inn.

In a few moments a boy came into the hall. He was not dressed like an ordinary hotel attendant, but his appearance was decent, and he might have been a sub-clerk or a head hall-boy.

"Can I obtain lodging here for the night?" I asked.

The boy looked at me from head to foot, and an expression such as might be produced by too much lemon juice came upon his face.

"No," said he; "we don't take cyclers."

This reception was something novel to me, who had cycled over thousands of miles, and I was not at all inclined to accept it at the hands of the boy. I stepped into the hall. "Can I see the master of this house?" said I.

"There ain't none," he answered, gruffly.

"Well, then, I want to see whoever is in charge."

He looked as if he were about to say that he was in charge, but he had no opportunity for such impertinence. A female figure came into the hall and advanced towards me. She stopped in an attitude of interrogation.

"I was just inquiring," I said, with a bow - for I saw that the new-comer was not a servant - "if I could be accommodated here for the night, but the boy informed me that cyclers are not received here."

"What!" she exclaimed, and turned as if she would speak to the boy, but he had vanished. "That is a mistake, sir," she said to me. "Very few wheelmen do stop here, as they prefer a hotel farther on, but we are glad to entertain them when they come."

It was not very light in the hall in which we stood, but I could see that this lady was young, that she was of medium size, and good-looking.

"Will you walk in, sir, and register?" she said. "I will have your wheel taken around to the back."

I followed her into a large apartment to the right of the hall - evidently a room of general assembly. Near the window was a desk with a great book on it. As I stood before this desk and she handed me a pen, her face was in the full light of the window, and glancing at it, the thought struck me that I now knew why Miss Putney did not wish me to stop at the Holly Sprig Inn. I almost laughed as I turned away my head to write my name. I was amused, and at the same time I could not help feeling highly complimented. It cannot but be grateful to the feelings of a young man to find that a very handsome woman objects to his making the acquaintance of an extremely pretty one.

When I laid down the pen she stepped up and looked at my name and address.

"Oh," said she, "you are the schoolmaster at Walford?" She seemed to be pleased by this discovery, and smiled in a very engaging way as she said, "I am much interested in that

school, for I received a great part of my education there."
"Indeed!" said I, very much surprised. "But I do not exactly understand. It is a boys' school."

"I know that," she answered, "but both boys and girls used to go there. Now the girls have a school of their own."

As she spoke I could not help contrasting in my mind what the school must have been with what it was now.

She stepped to the door and told a woman who was just entering the room to show me No. 2. The woman said something which I did not hear, although her tones indicated surprise, and then conducted me to my room.

This was an exceedingly pleasant chamber on the first floor at the back of the house. It was furnished far better than the quarters generally allotted to me in country inns, or, in fact, in hostelries of any kind. There was great comfort and even simple elegance in its appointments.

I would have liked to ask the maid some questions, but she was an elderly woman, who looked as if she might be the mother of the lemon-juice boy, and as she said not a word to me while she made a few arrangements in the room, I did not feel emboldened to say anything to her.

When I left my room and went out on the little porch, I soon came to the conclusion that this was not a house of great resort. I saw nobody in front and I heard nobody within. There seemed to be an air of quiet greenness about the surroundings, and the little porch was a charming place in which to sit and look upon the evening landscape.

After a time the boy came to tell me that supper was ready. He did so as if he were informing me that it was time to take medicine and he had just taken his.

Supper awaited me in a very pleasant room, through the open windows of which there came a gentle breeze which made me know that there was a flower-garden not far away. The table was a small one, round, and on it there was supper for one person. I seated myself, and the elderly woman waited on me. I was so grateful that the boy was not my attendant that my heart warmed towards her, and I thought she might not consider it much out of the way if I said something.

"Did I arrive after the regular supper-time?" I asked. "I am sorry if I put the establishment to any inconvenience."

"What's inconvenience in your own house isn't anything of the kind in a tavern," she said. "We're used to that. But it doesn't matter to-day. You're the only transient; that is, that eats here," she added.

I wanted very much to ask something about the lady who had gone to school in Walford, but I thought it would be well to approach that subject by degrees.

"Apparently," said I, "your house is not full."

"No," said she, "not at this precise moment of time. Do you want some more tea?"

The tone in which she said this made me feel sure she was the mother of the boy, and when she had given me the tea, and looked around in a general way to see that I was provided with what else I needed, she left the room.

After supper I looked into the large room where I had registered; it was lighted, and was very comfortably furnished with easy-chairs and a lounge, but it was an extremely lonely place, and, lighting a cigar, I went out for a walk. It was truly a beautiful country, and, illumined by the sunset sky, with all its forms and colors softened by the growing dusk, it was more charming to me than it had been by daylight.

As I returned to the inn I noticed a man standing at the entrance of a driveway which appeared to lead back to the stable-yards. "Here is some one who may talk," I thought, and I stopped.

"This ought to be a good country for sport," I said - "fishing, and that sort of thing."

"You're stoppin' here for the night?" he asked. I presumed from his voice and appearance that he was a stable-man, and from his tone that he was disappointed that I had not brought a horse with me.

I assented to his question, and he said:

"I never heard of no fishin'. When people want to fish, they go to a lake about ten miles furder on."

"Oh, I do not care particularly about fishing," I said, "but there must be a good many pleasant roads about here."

"There's this one," said he. "The people on wheels keep to it." With this he turned and walked slowly towards the back of the house.

"A lemon-loving lot!" thought I, and as I approached the porch I saw that the lady who had gone to school at Walford was standing there. I did not believe she had been eating lemons, and I stepped forward quickly for fear that she should depart before I reached her.

"Been taking a walk?" she said, pleasantly. There was something in the general air of this young woman which indicated that she should have worn a little apron with pockets, and that her hands should have been jauntily thrust into those pockets; but her dress included nothing of the sort.

The hall lamp was now lighted, and I could see that her attire was extremely neat and becoming. Her face was in shadow, but she had beautiful hair of a ruddy brown. I asked myself if she were the "lady clerk" of the establishment, or the daughter of the keeper of the inn. She was evidently a person in some authority, and one with whom it would be proper for me to converse, and as she had given me a very good opportunity to open conversation, I lost no time in doing so.

"And so you used to live in Walford?" I said.

"Oh yes," she replied, and then she began to speak of the pleasant days she had spent in that village. As she talked I endeavored to discover from her words who she was and what was her position. I did not care to discuss Walford. I wanted to talk about the Holly Sprig Inn, but I could not devise a courteous question which would serve my purpose.

Presently our attention was attracted by the sound of singing at the corner of the little lawn most distant from the house. It was growing dark, and the form of the singer could barely be discerned upon a bench under a great oak. The voice was that of a man, and his song was an Italian air from one of Verdi's operas. He sang in a low tone, as if he were simply amusing himself and did not wish to disturb the rest of the world.

"That must be the Italian who is stopping here for the night," she said. "We do not generally take such people; but he spoke so civilly, and said it was so hard to get lodging for his bear - "

"His bear!" I exclaimed.

"Oh yes," she answered, with a little laugh, "he has a bear with him. I suppose it dances, and so makes a living for its master. Anyway, I said he might stay and lodge with our stable-man. He would sing very well if he had a better voice - don't you think so?"

"We do not generally accommodate," "I said he might stay" - these were phrases which I turned over in my mind. If she were the lady clerk she might say "we" - even the boy said "we" - but "I said he might stay" was different. A daughter of a landlord or a landlady might say that.

I made a remark about the difficulty of finding lodging for man and beast, if the beast happened to be a bear, and I had scarcely finished it when from the house there came a shrill voice, flavored with lemon without any sugar, and it said, "Mrs. Chester!"

"Excuse me," said the young lady, and immediately she went in-doors.

Here was a revelation! Mrs. Chester! Strange to say, I had not thought of her as a married woman; and yet, now that I recalled her manner of perfect self-possession, she did suggest the idea of a satisfied young wife. And Mr. Chester - what of him? Could it be possible? Hardly. There was nothing about her to suggest a widow.

CHAPTER VII

MRS. CHESTER IS TROUBLED

I sat on that porch a good while, but she did not come out again. Why should she? Nobody came out, and within I could hear no sound of voices. I might certainly recommend this inn as a quiet place. The Italian and the crickets continued singing and chirping, but they only seemed to make the scene more lonely.

I went in-doors. On the left hand of the hall was a door which I had not noticed before, but which was now open. There was a light within, and I saw a prettily-furnished parlor. There was a table with a lamp on it, and by the table sat the lady, Mrs. Chester. I involuntarily stopped, and, looking up, she invited me to come in. Instantly I accepted the invitation, but with a sort of an apology for the intrusion.

"Oh, this is the public parlor," she said, "although everything about this house seems private at present. We generally have families staying with us in the summer, but last week nearly all of them went away to the sea-shore. In a few days, however, we expect to be full again."

She immediately began to talk about Walford, for evidently the subject interested her, and I answered all her questions as well as I could.

Frank R. Stockton

"You may know that my husband taught that school. I was his scholar before I became his wife."

I had heard of a Mr. Chester who, before me, had taught the school, but, although the information had not interested me at the time, now it did. I wished very much to ask what Mr. Chester was doing at present, but I waited.

"I went to boarding-school after I left Walford," said she, "and so for a time lost sight of the village, although I have often visited it since."

"How long is it since Mr. Chester gave up the school there?" I asked.

This proved to be a very good question indeed. "About six years," she said. "He gave it up just before we were married. He did not like teaching school, and as the death of his father put him into the possession of some money, he was able to change his mode of life. It was by accident that we settled here as innkeepers. We happened to pass the place, and Mr. Chester was struck by its beauty. It was not an inn then, but he thought it would make a charming one, and he also thought that this sort of life would suit him exactly. He was a student, a great reader, and a lover of rural sports - such as fishing and all that."

"Was." Here was a dim light. "Was" must mean that Mr. Chester had been. If he were living, he would still be a reader and a student.

"Did he find the new life all that he expected?" I said, hesitating a little at the word did, as it was not impossible that I might be mistaken.

"Oh yes, and more. I think the two years he spent here were the happiest of his life."

I was not yet quite sure about the state of affairs; he might be in an insane asylum, or he might be a hopeless invalid up-stairs.

"If he had lived," she continued, "I suppose this would have been a wonderfully beautiful place, for he was always making improvements. But it is four years now since his death, and in that time there has been very little change in the inn."

I do not remember what answer I made to this remark, but I gazed out upon the situation as if it were an unrolled map.

"When you wrote your name in the book," she said, "it seemed to me as if you had brought a note of introduction, and I am sure I am very glad to be acquainted with you, for, you know, you are my husband's successor. He did not like teaching, but he was fond of his scholars, and he always had a great fancy for school-teachers. Whenever one of them stopped here - which happened two or three times - he insisted that he should be put into our best room, if it happened to be vacant, and that is the reason I have put you into it to-day."

This was charming. She was such an extremely agreeable young person that it was delightful for me to think of myself in any way as her husband's successor.

There was a step at the door. I turned and saw the elderly servant.

"Mrs. Chester," she said, "I'm goin' up," and every word was flavored with citric acid.

"Good-night," said Mrs. Chester, taking up her basket and her work. "You know, you need not retire until you wish to do so. There is a room opposite, where gentlemen smoke."

I did not enter the big, lonely room. I went to my own chamber, which, I had just been informed, was the best in the house. I sat down in an easy-chair by the open window. I looked up to the twinkling stars.

Reading, studying, fishing, beautiful country, and all that. And he did not like school-teaching! No wonder he was happier here than he had ever been before! My eyes wandered around the tastefully furnished room. "Her husband's successor," I said to myself, pondering. "He did not like school-teaching, and he was so happy here." Of course he was happy. "Died and left him some money." There was no one to leave me any money, but I had saved some for the time when I should devote myself entirely to my profession. Profession - I thought. After all, what is there in a profession? Slavery; anxiety. And he chose a life of reading, studying, fishing, and everything else.

I turned to the window and again looked up into the sky. There was a great star up there, and it seemed to wink cheerfully at me as the words came into my mind, "her husband's successor."

When I opened my little valise, before going to bed, I saw the box the doctor's daughter had given me.

After sitting so long at the open window, thought I, it might be well to take one of these capsules, and I swallowed one.

When I was called to breakfast the next morning I saw that the table was laid with covers for two. In a moment my hostess entered and bade me good-morning. We sat down at the table; and the elderly woman waited. I could now see that her face was the color of a shop-worn lemon.

As for the lady who had gone to school at Walford - I wondered what place in the old school-room she had occupied - she was more charming than ever. Her manner was so cordial and cheerful that I could not doubt that she considered the entry of my name in her book as a regular introduction. She asked me about my plan of travel, how far I would go in a day, and that sort of thing. The elderly woman was very grim, and somehow or other I did not take very much interest in my plan of travel, but the meal was an extremely pleasant one for all that.

The natural thing for me to do after I finished my breakfast was to pay my bill and ride away, but I felt no inclination for anything of the sort. In fact, the naturalness of departure did not strike me. I went out on the little porch and gazed upon the bright, fresh morning landscape, and as I did so I asked myself why I should mount my bicycle and wheel away over hot and dusty roads, leaving all this cool, delicious beauty behind me.

What could I find more enjoyable than this? Why should I not spend a few days at this inn, reading, studying, fishing? Here I wondered why that man told me such a lie about the fishing. If I wanted to exercise on my wheel I felt sure there were pretty roads hereabout. I had plenty of time before me - my whole vacation. Why should I be consumed by this restless desire to get on?

I could not help smiling as I thought of my somewhat absurd fancies of the night before; but they were pleasant fancies, and I did not wonder that they had come to me. It certainly is provocative of pleasant fancies to have an exceedingly attractive young woman talk of you in any way as her husband's successor.

I could not make up my mind what I ought to do, and I walked back into the hall. I glanced into the parlor, but it was unoccupied. Then I went into the large room on the right; no one was there, and I stood by the window trying to make up

Frank R. Stockton

my mind in regard to proposing a brief stay at the inn.

It really did not seem necessary to give the matter much thought. Here was a place of public entertainment, and, as I was one of the public, why should I not be entertained? I had stopped at many a road-side hostelry, and in each one of them I knew I would be welcome to stay as long as I was willing to pay.

Still, there was something, some sort of an undefined consciousness, which seemed to rise in the way of an off-hand proposal to stay at this inn for several days, when I had clearly stated that I wished to stop only for the night.

While I was still turning over this matter in my mind Mrs. Chester came into the room. I had expected her. The natural thing for her to do was to come in and receive the amount I owed her for her entertainment of me, but as I looked at her I could not ask her for my bill. It seemed to me that such a thing would shock her sensibilities. Moreover, I did not want her bill.

It was plain enough, however, that she expected me to depart, for she asked me where I proposed to stop in the middle of the day, and she suggested that she should have a light luncheon put up for me. She thought probably a wheelman would like that sort of thing, for then he could stop and rest wherever it suited him.

"Speaking of stopping," said I, "I am very glad that I did not do as I was advised to do and go on to the Cheltenham. I do not know anything about that hotel, but I am sure it is not so charming as this delightful little inn with its picturesque surroundings."

"I am glad you did not," she answered. "Who advised you to go on to the Cheltenham?"

"Miss Putney," said I. "Her father's place is between here and Walford. I stopped there night before last." And then, as I was glad of an opportunity to prolong the interview, I told her the history of my adventures at that place.

Mrs. Chester was amused, and I thought I might as well tell her how I came to be delayed on the road and so caught in the storm, and I related my experience with Miss Burton. I would have been glad to go still farther back and tell her how I came to take the school at Walford, and anything else she might care to listen to.

When I told her about Miss Burton she sat down in a chair near by and laughed heartily.

"It is wonderfully funny," she said, "that you should have met those two young ladies and should then have stopped here."

"You know them?" I said, promptly taking another chair.

"Oh yes," she answered. "I know them both; and, as I have mentioned that your meeting with them seemed funny to me, I suppose I ought to tell you the reason. Some time ago a photographer in Walford, who has taken a portrait of me and also of Miss Putney and Miss Burton, took it into his head to print the three on one card and expose them for sale with a ridiculous inscription under them. This created a great deal of talk, and Miss Putney made the photographer destroy his negative and all the cards he had on hand. After that we were talked about as a trio, and, I expect, a good deal of fun was made of us. And now it seems a little odd - does it not? - that you have become acquainted with all the members of this trio as soon as you left Walford. But I must not keep you in this way." And she rose.

Now was my opportunity to make known my desire to be

kept, but before I could do so the boy hurriedly came into the room.

"The Dago wants to see you," he said. "He's in an awful hurry."

"Excuse me," said Mrs. Chester. "It is that Italian who was singing outside last night. I thought he had gone. Would you mind waiting a few minutes?"

It was getting harder and harder to enunciate my proposition to make a sojourn at the inn. I wished that I had spoken sooner. It is so much easier to do things promptly.

While I was waiting the elderly woman came in. "Do you want the boy to take your little bag out and strap it on?" said she.

Evidently there was no want of desire to speed the departing guest. "Oh, I will attend to that myself," said I, but I made no step to do it. When my hostess came back I wanted to be there.

Presently she did come back. She ran in hurriedly, and her face was flushed. "Here is a very bad piece of business," she said. "That man's bear has eaten the tire off one of your wheels!"

"What!" I exclaimed, and my heart bounded within me. Here, perhaps, was the solution of all my troubles. If by any happy chance my bicycle had been damaged, of course I could not go on.

"Come and see," she said, and, following her through the back hall door, we entered a large, enclosed yard. Not far from the house was a shed, and in front of this lay my bicycle on its side in an apparently disabled condition. An

Italian, greatly agitated, was standing by it. He was hatless, and his tangled black hair hung over his swarthy face. At the other end of the yard was a whitish-brown bear, not very large, and chained to a post.

I approached my bicycle, earnestly hoping that the bear had been attempting to ride it, but I found that he had been trying to do something very different. He had torn the pneumatic tire from one of the wheels, and nearly the whole of it was lying scattered about in little bits upon the ground.

"How did this happen?" I said to the Italian, feeling very much inclined to give him a dollar for the good offices of the beast.

The man began immediately to pour out an explanation upon me. His English was as badly broken as the torn parts of my tire, but I had no trouble in understanding. The bear had got loose in the night. He had pulled up a little post to which he had been chained. The man had not known it was such a weak post. The bear was never muzzled at night. He had gone about looking for something to eat. He was very fond of India-rubber - or, as the man called it, "Injer-rub." He always ate up India-rubber shoes wherever he could find them. He would eat them off a man's feet if the man should be asleep. He liked the taste of Injer-rub. He did not swallow it. He dropped it all about in little bits.

Then the man sprang towards me and seized the injured wheel. "See!" he exclaimed. "He eat your Injer-rub, but he no break your machine!"

This was very true. The wheel did not seem to be injured, but still I could not travel without a tire. This was the most satisfactory feature of the affair. If he and I had been alone together I would have handed the man two dollars, and told him to go in peace with his bear and give himself no more trouble.

But we were not alone. The stable-man who had lied to me about the fishing was there; the boy who had lied to me about the reception of cyclers was there; the lemon-faced woman was there, standing close to Mrs. Chester; and there were two maids looking out of the window of the kitchen.

"This is very bad indeed!" said Mrs. Chester, addressing the Italian. "You have damaged this gentleman's wheel, and you must pay him for it."

Now the Italian began to tear his hair. Never before had I seen any one tear his hair. More than that, he shed tears, and declared he had no money. After he had paid his bill he would not have a cent in the world. His bear had ruined him. He was in despair.

"What are you going to do?" said Mrs. Chester to me. "You cannot use your bicycle."

Before I could answer, the elderly woman exclaimed: "You ought to come in, Mrs. Chester! This is no place for you! Suppose that beast should break loose again! Let the gentle-man settle it with the man."

I do not think my hostess wanted to go, but she accompanied her grim companion into the house.

"I suppose there is no place near here where I can have a new tire put on this wheel?" said I to the stable-man.

"Not nearer than Waterton," he replied; "but we could take you and your machine there in a wagon."

"That's so," said the boy. "I'll drive."

I glared upon the two fellows as if they had been a couple of fiends who were trying to put a drop of poison into my cup of joy. To be dolefully driven to Waterton by that boy! What a picture! How different from my picture!

The Italian sat down on the ground and embraced his knees with his arms. He moaned and groaned, and declared over and over again that he was ruined; that he had no money to pay.

In regard to him my mind was made up. I would forgive him his debt and send him away with my blessing, even if I found no opportunity of rewarding him for his great service to me.

I would go in and speak to Mrs. Chester about it. Of course it would not be right to do anything without consulting her, and now I could boldly tell her that it would suit me very well to stop at the inn until my wheel could be sent away and repaired.

As I entered the large room the elderly woman came out. She was plainly in a bad humor. Mrs. Chester was awaiting me with an anxious countenance, evidently much more troubled about the damage to my bicycle than I was. I hastened to relieve her mind.

"It does not matter a bit about the damage done by the bear," I said. "I should not wonder if that wheel would be a great deal better for a new tire, anyway. And, as for that doleful Italian, I do not want to be hard on him, even if he has a little money in his pocket."

But my remarks did not relieve her, while my cheerful and contented tones seemed to add to her anxiety.

"But you cannot travel," she said, "and there is no place about here where you could get a new tire."

It was very plain that no one in this house entertained the idea that it would be a good thing for me to rest here quietly until my bicycle could be sent away and repaired. In fact, my first statement, that I wished to stop but for the night, was accepted with general approval.

I did not deem it necessary to refer to the man's offer, to send me and my machine to Waterton in a wagon, and I was just on the point of boldly announcing that I was in no hurry whatever to get on, and that it would suit me very well to wait here for a few days, when the boy burst into the room, one end of his little neck-tie flying behind him.

"The Dago's put!" he shouted. "He's put off and gone!"

We looked at him in amazement.

"Gone!" I exclaimed. "Shall I go after him? Has he paid his bill?"

"No, you needn't do that," said the boy. "He cut across the fields like a chipmunk - skipped right over the fences! You'd never ketch him, and you needn't try! He's off for the station. I'll tell you all about it," said the boy, turning to his mistress, who had been too much startled to ask any questions. "When he went into the house" - jerking his head in my direction - "I was left alone with the Dago, and he begun to talk to me. He asked me a lot of things. He rattled on so I couldn't understand half he said. He wanted to know how much a tire cost; he wanted to know how much his bill would be, and if he'd have to pay for the little post that was broke.

"Then he asked if I thought that if he'd promise to send you the money would the gentleman let him go without payin' for the tire, and he wanted to know what your name was; and when I told him you hadn't no husband, and what your name was, he asked me to say it over again, and then he made me say it once more - the whole of it; and while I was tellin' him that I'd write it down for him if he wanted to send you the money, he give a big jump and he stuck his head out like a bull. He looked so queer that I was gettin' skeered; and then he says, almost whisperin': 'I go! I go away! I leave my bear! If she sell him, that pay everything! I come back no more - never! never!'

"I saw he was goin' to scoot, and I made a grab at him, but he give me a push that nearly tore my collar off, and away he went. You never see anybody run like he run. He was out of sight in no time."

"And he left his bear!" she exclaimed, in horror. "What on earth am I to do with a bear?" She looked at me, and in spite of her annoyance and perplexity she could not help joining me when I laughed outright.

CHAPTER VIII

ORSO

Mrs. Chester and I hurried back to the yard. There was the bear, sitting calmly on his haunches, but there was no Italian.

"Now that his master is gone," my hostess exclaimed, "I am afraid of him! I will not go any farther! Can you imagine anything that can be done with that beast?"

I had no immediate answer to give, and I was still very much amused at the absurdity of the situation. Had any one ever before paid his bill in such fashion? At this moment the stable-man approached us from one of the outbuildings. "This is my hostler," she said. "Perhaps he can suggest something."

"This is a bad go, ma'am," said he. "The horse was out in the pasture all night, but this morning when I went to bring him up I couldn't make him come near the stable. He smells that bear! It seems to drive him crazy!"

"It's awful!" she said. "What are we going to do, John? Do you think the animal will become dangerous when he misses his master?"

"Oh, there's nothin' dangerous about him," answered John. "I was sittin' talkin' to that Dago last night after supper, and he says his bear's tamer than a cat. He is so mild-tempered that he wouldn't hurt nobody. The Dago says he sleeps close up to him of cold nights to keep himself warm. There ain't no trouble about his bein' dangerous, but you can't bring the horse into the stable while he's about. If anybody was to drive into this yard without knowin' they'd be a circus, I can tell you! Horses can't stand bears."

She looked at me in dismay. "Couldn't he be shot and buried?" she asked.

I had my doubts on that point. A tame bear is a valuable animal, and I could not advise her to dispose of the property of another person in that summary way.

"But he must be got away," she said. "We can't have a bear here. He must be taken away some way or other. Isn't there any place where he could be put until the Italian comes back?"

"That Dago's never comin' back," said the boy, solemnly. "If you'd a-seen him scoot, you'd a-knowed that he was dead skeered, and would never turn up here no more, bear or no bear."

Mrs. Chester looked at me. She was greatly worried, but she was also amused, and she could not help laughing.

"Isn't this a dreadful predicament?" she said. "What in the world am I to do?" At this moment there was an acidulated voice from the kitchen. "Mrs. Whittaker wants to see you, Mrs. Chester," it cried, "right away!"

"Oh, dear!" said she. "Here is more trouble! Mrs. Whittaker is an invalid lady who is so nervous that she could not sleep one night because she heard a man had killed a snake at the back of the barn, and what she will say when she hears that we have a bear here without a master I do not know. I must go to her, and I do wish you could think of something that I can do;" as she said this she looked at me as if it were a natural thing for her to rely upon me. For a moment it made me think of the star that had winked the night before.

Mrs. Chester hurried into the house, and in company with the stable-man I crossed the yard towards the bear.

"You are sure he is gentle?" said I.

"Mild as milk!" said the man. "I was a-playin' with him last night. He'll let you do anything with him! If you box his ears, he'll lay over flat down on his side!"

When we were within a few feet of the bear he sat upright, dangled his fore paws in front of him, and, with his head on one side, he partly opened his mouth and lolled out his tongue. "I guess he's beggin' for his breakfust," said John.

"Can't you get him something to eat?" I asked. "He ought to be fed, to begin with."

The man went back to the kitchen, and I walked slowly around the bear, looking at the chain and the post, and trying to see what sort of a collar was almost hidden under his shaggy hair. Apparently he seemed securely attached, and then - as he was at the end of his chain - I went up to him and gently patted one paw. He did not object to this, and turning his head he let his tongue loll out on the other side, fixing his little black eyes upon me with much earnestness. When the man came with the pan of scraps from the kitchen I took it from him and placed it on the ground in front of the bear. Instantly the animal dropped to his feet and began to eat with earnest rapidity.

"I wonder how much he'd take in for one meal," said John, "if you'd give him all he wanted? I guess that Dago never let him have any more'n he could help."

As the bear was licking the tin pan I stood and looked at him. "I wonder if he would be tame with strangers?" said I. "Do you suppose we could take him away from this post if we wanted to?"

"Oh yes," said John. "I wouldn't be afraid to take him anywheres, only there isn't any place to take him to." He then stepped quite close to the bear. "Hey, horsey!" said he. "Hey, old horsey! Good old horsey!"

"Is that his name?" I asked.

"That's what the Dago called him," said John. "Hey, horsey! Good horsey!" And he stooped and unfastened the chain from the post.

I imagined that the Italian had called the bear "Orso," perhaps with some diminutive, but I did not care to discuss this. I was very much interested to see what the man was going to do. With the end of the chain in his hand, John now stepped in front of the bear and said, "Come along, horsey!" and, to my surprise, the bear began to shamble after him as quietly as if he had been following his old master. "See!" cried John. "He'll go anywheres I choose to take him!" and he began to lead him about the yard.

As he approached the kitchen there came a fearful scream from the open window.

"Take him away! Take him away!" I heard, in the shrillest accents.

"They're dreadfully skeered," said John, as he led the bear

back; "but he wouldn't hurt nobody! It would be a good thing, though, to put his muzzle on; that's it hangin' over there by the shed; it's like a halter, and straps up his jaws. The Dago said there ain't no need for it, but he puts it on when he's travellin' along the road to keep people from bein' skeered."

"It would be well to put it on," said I. "I wonder if we can get him into it?"

"I guess he'd let you do anything you'd a mind to,'' replied John, as he again fastened the chain to the post.

I took down the muzzle and approached the bear. He did not growl, but stood perfectly still and looked at me. I put the muzzle over his head, and, holding myself in readiness to elude a sudden snap, I strapped up his jaws. The creature made no snap - he gazed at me with mild resignation.

"As far as he goes," said John, "he's all right; but as far as everything else goes - especially horses - they're all wrong. He's got to be got rid of some way."

I had nothing more to say to John, and I went into the house. I met Mrs. Chester in the hall.

"I have had a bad time up-stairs," she said. "Mrs. Whittaker declares that she will not stay an hour in a house where there is a bear without a master; but as she has a terrible sciatica and cannot travel, I do not know what she is going to do. Her trained nurse, I believe, is now putting on her bonnet to depart."

As she spoke, the joyful anticipation of a few days at the Holly Sprig Inn began to fade away. I did not blame the bear as the present cause of my disappointment. He had done all he could for me. It was his wretched master who had done the mischief by running away and leaving him. But no matter what had happened, I saw my duty plainly before me. I had not been encouraged to stay, but it is possible that I might have done so without encouragement, but now I saw that I must go. The Fates, who, as I had hoped, had compelled my stay, now compelled my departure.

"Do not give yourself another thought upon the subject," I said. "I will settle the whole matter, and nobody need be frightened or disturbed. The Cheltenham Hotel is only a few miles farther on, and I shall have to walk there anyway. I will start immediately and take the bear with me. I am sure that he will allow me to lead him wherever I please. I have tried him, and I find that he is a great deal gentler than most children."

She exclaimed, in horror: "You must not think of it! He might spring upon you and tear you to pieces!"

"Oh, he will not do that," I answered. "He is not that sort of a bear - and, besides, he is securely muzzled. I muzzled him myself, and he did not mind it in the least. Oh, you need not be afraid of the bear; he has had his breakfast and he is in perfect good-humor with the world. It will not take me long to reach the hotel, and I shall enjoy the walk, and when I get there I will be sure to find some shed or out-house where the beast can be shut up until it can be decided what to do with him. I can leave him there and have him legally advertised, and then - if nothing else can be done - he can be shot. I shall be very glad to have his skin; it will be worth enough to cover his bill here, and the damages to my bicycle. I shall send for that as soon as I reach the hotel. I can go to Waterton by train and take it with me. I can have it made all right in Waterton. So now, you see, I have settled everything satisfactorily."

She looked at me earnestly, and, although there was a certain

Frank R. Stockton

solitude in her gaze, I could also see there signs of great relief. "But isn't there some other way of getting that bear to the hotel?" she said. "It will be dreadful for you to have to walk there and lead him."

"It's the only way to do it," I answered. "You could not hitch a bear behind a wagon - the horse would run away and jerk his head off. The only way to take a bear about the country is to lead him, and I do not mind it in the least. As I have got to go without my bicycle I would like to have some sort of company. Anyway, the bear must go, and as I am on the road to the Cheltenham I shall be very glad to take him along with me."

"I think you are wonderfully brave," she said, "and very good. If I can persuade myself it will be perfectly safe for you, it will certainly be a great relief to me."

I was now engaged in a piece of self-sacrifice, and I felt that I must do it thoroughly and promptly. "I will go and get my valise," I said, "for I ought to start immediately."

"Oh, I will send that!" she exclaimed.

"No," I answered; "it does not weigh anything, and I can sling it over my shoulder. By-the-way," I said, turning as I was about to leave the room, "I have forgotten something." I put my hand into my pocket; it would not do to forget that I was, after all, only a departing guest.

"No, no," she replied, quickly, "I am your debtor. When you find out how much damage you have suffered, and what is to be done with the bear, all that can be settled. You can write to me, but I will have nothing to do with it now."

With my valise over my shoulder I returned to the hall to take leave of my hostess. Now she seemed somewhat contrite. Fate and she had conquered, I was going away, and she was sorry for me.

"I think it is wonderfully good of you to do all this," she said. "I wish I could do something for you."

I would have been glad to suggest that she might ask me to come again, and it would also have pleased me to say that I did not believe that her husband, if he could express his opinion, would commend her apparent inhospitality to his successor. But I made no such remarks, and offered my hand, which she cordially clasped as if I were an old friend and were going away to settle in the Himalayas.

I went into the yard to get Orso. He was lying down when I approached him, but I think he knew from my general appearance that I was prepared to take the road, and he rose to his feet as much as to say, "I am ready." I unfastened the chain from the post, and, with the best of wishes for good-luck from John, who now seemed to be very well satisfied with me, I walked around the side of the house, the bear following as submissively as if he had been used to my leadership all his life.

I did not see the boy nor the lemon-faced woman, and I was glad of it. I believe they would have cast evil eyes upon me, and there is no knowing what that bear might have done in consequence.

Mrs. Chester was standing in the door as I reached the road. "Good-bye!" she cried, "and good fortune go with you!" I raised my hat, and gave Orso a little jerk with the chain.

CHAPTER IX

A RUNAWAY

He was a very slow walker, that bear. If I had been alone I would have been out of sight of the inn in less than five minutes. As it was, I looked back after a considerable time to see if I really were out of sight of the house, and I found I was not. She was still standing in the doorway, and when I turned she waved her handkerchief. Now that I had truly left and was gone, she seemed to be willing to let me know better than before what a charming woman she was. I took off my hat again and pressed forward.

For a couple of miles, perhaps, I walked thoughtfully, and I do not believe I once thought of the bear shambling silently behind me. I had been dreaming a day-dream - not building a castle in the air, for I had seen before me a castle already built. I had simply been dreaming myself into it, into its life, into its possessions, into the possession of everything which belonged to it.

It had been a fascinating vision. It had suited my fancy better than any vision of the future which I had ever had. I was not ambitious; I loved the loveliness of life. I was a student, and I had a dream of life which would not interfere with the society of my books. I loved all rural pleasures, and I had dreamed of a life where these were spread out ready for my enjoyment. I was a man formed to love, and there had come to me dreams of this sort of thing.

My dreams had even taken practical shape. As I was dressing myself that morning I had puzzled my brain to find a pretext for taking the first step, which would be to remain a few days at the inn.

The pretext for doing this had appeared to me. For a moment I had snatched at it and shown my joy, and then it had utterly disappeared - the vision, the fancy, the anticipations, the plans, the vine-covered home in the air, all were destroyed as completely as if it had been the tire of my bicycle scattered about in little bits upon the ground.

"Come along, old Orso!" I exclaimed, endeavoring to mend my pace, and giving the bear a good pull upon his chain. But the ugly creature did not walk any faster; he simply looked at me with an air as if he would say that if I kept long upon the road I would learn to take it easy, and maintained the deliberate slouch of his demeanor.

Presently I stopped, and Orso was very willing to imitate me in that action. I found, to my surprise, that I was not walking upon a macadamized road: such was the highway which passed the inn and led, I had been told, to the Cheltenham. I was now upon a road of gravel and clay, smooth enough and wide enough, but of a different character from that on which I had started that morning. I looked about me. Across a field to my left I saw a line of trees which seemed to indicate a road. I had a dim recollection of having passed a road which seemed to turn to the left, but I had been thinking very earnestly, and had paid little attention to it. Probably that road was the main road and this the one which turned off.

I determined to investigate. It would not do to wander out of my way with my present encumbrance. It was now somewhat after noon; the country people were eating their dinners or engaged about their barns; there was nobody upon the road. At some distance ahead of me was a small house standing well back behind a little group of trees. and I decided to go there and make inquiries. And as it would not do at all to throw a rural establishment into a state of wild confusion by leading a bear up to its door, I conducted Orso to the side of the road and chained him to a fence-post. He was perfectly satisfied and lay down, his nose upon his fore-paws.

I found three women in the little house. They were in a side kitchen eating their dinner, and I wondered what the bear would have done if he had smelled that dinner. They told me that I was not on the main road, and would have to go back more than half a mile in order to regain it.

When I was out on the road again I said to myself that if I could possibly make Orso step along at a little more lively pace I might get to the hotel in time for a very late luncheon, and I was beginning to think that I had not been wise in declining portable refreshment, when I heard a noise ahead of me. At a considerable distance along the road, and not far from where I had left the bear, I saw a horse attached to a vehicle approaching me at a furious speed. He was running away! The truth flashed upon me - he had been frightened by Orso!

I ran a few steps towards the approaching horse. His head was high in the air, and the vehicle swayed from side to side. It was a tall affair with two wheels, and on the high seat sat a lady vainly tugging at the reins. My heart sank. What dreadful thing had I done!

I stood in the middle of the road. It seemed but a few seconds before the horse was upon me. He swerved to one side, but I was ready for that. I dashed at his bridle, but caught the end of his cumbrous bit in my right hand. I leaned forward with all the strength that dwelt in my muscles and nerves. The horse's glaring eye was over my face, and I felt the round end of a shaft rise up under my arm. A pair of outstretched forelegs slid past me. I saw the end of a banged tail switching in the dust. The horse was on his haunches. He was stopped.

Before I had time to recover an erect attitude and to let up the horse the occupant of the vehicle was on the ground She had skipped down with wonderful alacrity on the side opposite to me, and was coming round by the back of the cart. The horse was now standing on his four legs, trembling in every fibre, and with eyes that were still wild and staring. Holding him firmly, I faced the lady as she stopped near me. She was a young woman in a jaunty summer costume and a round straw hat. She did not seem to be quite mistress of herself; she was not pale, but perhaps that was because her face was somewhat browned by the sun, but her step was not steady, and she breathed hard. Under ordinary circumstances she would have been assisted to the side of the road, where she might sit down and recover herself, and have water brought to her. But I could do nothing of that sort. I could not leave that shivering horse.

"Are you hurt?" I asked.

"Oh no," she said, "but I am shaken up a bit. I cannot tell you how grateful I am! I don't believe I ever can tell you!"

"Do not speak of that." I said, quickly. "Perhaps you would feel better if you were to sit down somewhere."

"Oh, I don't want to sit down," said she. "I am so glad to have my feet on the solid earth again that that is enough for me. It was a bear that frightened him - a bear lying down by the side of the road a little way back. He never ran away before, but when he saw that bear he gave a great shy and a bolt, and he was off. I just got a glimpse of the beast."

I was very anxious to change the conversation, and suggested that I lead the horse into the shade, for the sun was blazing down upon us. The horse submitted to be led to the side of the road, but he was very nervous, and looked everywhere for the approach of shaggy bears.

"It is perfectly dreadful," she said, when she again approached me, "for people to leave bears about in that way. I suppose he was fastened, for it could not have been a wild beast. They do not lie down by the side of the road. I do not say that I was rattled, but I expected every second that there would be a smash, and there would have been if it had not been for - "

"It is a wonder you were not thrown out," I interrupted, "those carts are so tall."

"Yes," she answered, "and if I hadn't slipped off the driving-cushion at the first shy I would have been out sure. I never had anything happen like this, but who could have expected a great bear by the side of the road?"

"Have you far to go?" I asked.

"Not very - about three miles. I made a call this morning on the other road, and was driving home. My name is Miss Larramie. My father's place is on this road. He is Henry Esmond Larramie." I had heard of the gentleman, but had never met him. "I am not afraid of horses," she continued, "but I do not know about driving this one now. He looks as if he were all ready to bolt again."

"Oh, it would not do for you to drive him," I said. "That would be extremely risky."

"I might walk home," she said, "but I could not leave the horse."

"Let me think a minute," said I. Then presently I asked, "Will this horse stand if he is hitched?"

"Oh yes," she answered; "I always hitch him when I make calls. There is a big strap under the seat which goes around his neck, and then through a ring in his bit. He has to stand - he can't get away."

"Very well, then," said I; "I will tell you what I will do. I will tie him to this tree. I think he is quieter, and if you will stand by him and talk to him - he knows you?"

"Oh yes," she answered, "and I can feed him with grass. But why do you want to tie him? What are you going to do?"

As she spoke she brought me the tie strap, and I proceeded to fasten the horse to a tree.

"Now, then," said I, "I must go and get the bear and take him away somewhere out of sight. It will never do to leave him there. Some other horse might be coming along."

"You get the bear!" she said, surprised.

"Yes," I answered; "he is my bear, and - "

She stepped back, her eyes expanded and her lower jaw dropped. "*Your* bear!" she cried, and with that her glance seemed to run all over me as if she were trying to find some resemblance to a man who exhibited a bear.

"Yes," I replied; "I left him there while I went to ask my way. It was a dreadful thing to do, but I must leave him there no longer. I will tell you all about it when I come back."

Frank R. Stockton

I had decided upon a plan of action. I ran down the road to the bear, took down some bars of the fence, and then, untying him, I led him over a field to a patch of woodland. Orso shuffled along humbly as if it did not make any difference to him where he went, and when I reached the woods I entered it by an old cart-road, and soon struck off to one side among some heavy underbrush. Finding a spot where it would be impossible for the beast to be seen from the road, I fastened him securely to a tree. He looked after me regretfully, and I think I heard him whine, but I am not sure of that. I hurried back to the road, replaced the bars, and very soon had joined the young lady.

"Well," said she, "never in this world would I have thought that was your bear! But what is to be done now? This horse gave a jump as soon as he heard you running this way."

"Now," said I, "I will drive you to your house, or, if you are afraid, you can walk, and I will take him home for you if you will give me the directions."

"Oh, I am not a bit afraid," she said. "I am sure you can manage him - you seem to be able to manage animals. But will not this be a great inconvenience to you? Are you going this way? And won't you have to come back after your bear? I can't believe that you are really leading a bear about."

I laughed as I unfastened the horse. "It will not take me long to come back," I said. "Now, I will get in first, and, when I have him properly in hand, you can mount on the other side."

The young lady appeared to have entirely recovered from the effects of her fright, and was by my side in a moment. The horse danced a little as we started and tried to look behind him, but he soon felt that he was under control, and trotted off finely.

I now thought that I ought to tell her who I was, for I did not want to be taken for a travelling showman, although I really did not suppose that she would make such a mistake.

"So you are the school-master at Walford!" said she. "I have heard about you. Little Billy Marshall is one of your scholars."

I admitted that he was, and that I was afraid he did not do me very much credit.

"Perhaps not," she said, "but he is a good boy. His mother sometimes works for us; she does quite heavy jobs of sewing, and Billy brings them up by train. He was here a little more than a week ago, and I asked him how he was getting on at school, and if he had a good teacher, and he said the man was pretty good. But I want to know about the bear. How in the world did you happen to be leading a bear?"

I related the ursine incident, which amused her very much, and, as she was a wheelwoman herself, she commiserated with me sincerely on the damage to my machine.

"So you stopped at the Holly Sprig?" she said. "And how did you like the mistress of that little inn?"

I replied that I had found her very interesting.

"Yes, she is an interesting woman," said my companion, "and a very pretty one, too. Some people wonder why she continues to keep the inn, but perhaps she has to. You know, her husband was murdered."

"No, I did not!" I exclaimed, in surprise. "I knew he was not living - but murdered! That is dreadful! How did that happen?"

"Nobody knows," she answered. "They had not been married very long - I do not know how long - when he was killed. He went to New York on business by himself, and did not come back. They were searching for him days and days - ever so long, and they could find no clew. At last - it may have been a month afterwards - or perhaps it was more - it was found that he had been murdered. His body had been discovered, and was supposed to be that of somebody else, and had been buried in whatever place the authorities buried people in such cases. Then it was too late to get it or to identify it, or to do anything. Wasn't that perfectly awful?"

This story gave me a peculiar shock. I could not have imagined that that charming and apparently light-hearted young woman at the Holly Sprig had ever been crushed down by such a sorrow as this. But I did not ask any more questions. The young girl by my side probably knew no more than she had already told me. Besides, I did not want to hear any more.

"'Royal' goes along just as if nothing had happened," she said, admiringly regarding the horse. "Now, I wonder if it will be safe for me to drive him again?"

"I should be very sorry," I answered, "if my thoughtlessness had rendered him unsafe for you; but if he could be led up and down past the place where he saw the bear until he becomes convinced that there is now nothing dreadful in that spot, he may soon be all right again."

"Do you know," she said, suddenly turning towards me, "what I would like better than anything else in this world? I would like to be able to stand in the middle of the road and stop a horse as you did!"

I laughed and assured her that I knew there were a great many things in the world which it would be much better for her to do than that.

"Nothing would please me so much," she said, decisively, "not one single, solitary thing! There's our gate. Turn in here, please."

I drove up a winding road which led to a house standing among trees on a slight elevation. "Please let me out here," she said, when I reached the end of the porch. "I will send a man to take the horse."

CHAPTER X

THE LARRAMIE FAMILY

I think I did not have to wait ten seconds after her departure, for a stable-man had seen us approach and immediately came forward. I jumped down from the cart and looked in the direction of the road. I thought if I were to make a cross-cut over the lawn and some adjacent fields I should get back to my bear much quicker than if I returned the way I had come. But this thought had scarcely shaped itself in my mind when I heard the approach of hurrying feet, and in the next moment a little army had thrown itself upon me.

There was a tall, bright-faced man, with side whiskers and a flowing jacket, who came forward with long steps and outstretched hand; there was a lady behind him, with little curls on the side of her head; and there were some boys and girls and other people. And nearly in front of the whole of them was the young lady I had brought to the house. Each one of them seized me by the hand; each one of them told me what a great thing I had done; each of them thanked me from the bottom of his or her heart for saving the life of his or her daughter or sister, and not one of them gave me a chance to say that as I had done all the mischief I could not be too thankful that I had been able to avert evil consequences. From the various references to the details of the incident I concluded that the young lady had dashed into the house and had given a full account of everything which had happened in less time than it would have taken me to arrange my ideas for such a recital.

As soon as I could get a chance I thanked them all for their gracious words, and said that as I was in a hurry I must take my leave. Thereupon arose a hubbub of voices. "Not at dinner-time!" exclaimed Mr. Larramie. "We would never listen to such a thing!"

"And you need not trouble yourself about your bear," cried my young lady, whose Christian name I soon discovered to be Edith. "He can live on barks and roots until we have time to attend to him. He is used to that in his native wilds."

Now everybody wanted to know everything about the bear, and great was the hilarity which my account occasioned.

"Come in! Come in!" exclaimed Mr. Larramie. "The bear will be all right if you tied him well. You have just time to get ready for dinner." And noticing a glance I had given to my garments, he continued: "You need not bother about your clothes. We are all in field costume. Oh, I did not see you had a valise. Now, hurry in, all of you!"

That dinner was a most lively meal. Everybody seemed to be talking at once, yet they all found time to eat. The father talked so much that his daughter Edith took the carving-fork from him and served out the mutton-chops herself. The mother, from the other end of the table, with tears in her eyes, continually asked me if I would not have something or other, and how I could ever screw up my courage to go about with an absolutely strange bear.

There was a young man, apparently the oldest son, with a fine, frank manner and very broad shoulders. He was so wonderfully developed about the bust that he seemed almost deformed, his breast projecting so far that it gave him the appearance of being round-shouldered in front. This, my practised eye told me, was the result of undue exercise in the direction of chest-expansion. He was a good-natured fellow, and overlooked my not answering several of his questions, owing to the evident want of opportunity to do so.

There was a yellow-haired girl with a long plait down her back; there was a half-grown boy, wearing a blue calico shirt with a red cravat; there was a small girl who sat by her mother; and there was a young lady, very upright and slender, who did not seem to belong to the family, for she never used the words "father" and "mother," which were continually in the mouths of the others. This young lady talked incessantly, and fired her words after the manner of a Gatling gun, without taking aim at anybody in particular. Sometimes she may have been talking to me, but, as she did not direct her gaze towards me on such occasions, I did not feel bound to consider any suppositions in regard to the matter.

I, of course, was the principal object of general attention. They wanted to know what I really thought of Billy Marshall as a scholar. They wanted to know if I would have some more. They wanted to know if I had had any previous experience with bears. The father asked which I thought it would be easier to manage, a boy or a bear. The boy Percy wanted to know how I placed my feet when I stood up in front of a runaway horse. Others asked if I intended to go back to my school at Walford, and how I liked the village, and if I were president of the literary society there, which Mrs. Larramie thought I ought to be, on account of my scholastic position.

But before the meal was over the bear had come to be the absorbing subject of conversation. I was asked my plans about him, and they were all disapproved.

"It would be of no use to take him to the Cheltenham," said Walter, the oldest son. "They couldn't keep him there. They have too many horses - a livery-stable. They wouldn't let you come on the place with him."

"Of course not," said Mr. Larramie. "And, besides, why should you take him there? It would be a poor place anyway. They wouldn't keep him until his owner turned up. They wouldn't have anything to do with him. What you want to do is to bring your bear here. We have a hay-barn out in the fields. He could sleep in the hay, and we could give him a long chain so that he could have a nice range."

The younger members of the family were delighted with this suggestion. Nothing would please them better than to have a bear on the place. Each one of them was ready to take entire charge of it, and Percy declared that he would go into the woods and hunt for wild-bee honey with which to feed it. Even Mrs. Larramie assured me that if a bear were well chained, at a suitable distance, she would have no fears whatever of it.

I accepted the proposition, for I was glad to get rid of the animal in a way which would please so many people, and after dinner was over, and I had smoked a cigar with my host and his son Walter, I said that it was time for me to go and get the bear.

"But you won't go by the main road," said Mr. Larramie. "That makes a great curve below here to avoid a hill. If I understood you properly, you left the bear not far from a small house inhabited by three women?"

"They're the McKenna sisters," added Walter.

"Yes," said the father, "and their house is not more than two miles from here by a field road. I will go with you."

Frank R. Stockton

I exclaimed that I would not put him to so much trouble, but my words were useless. The Walter son declared that he would go also, that he would like the walk; the Percy son declared he was going if anybody went; and Genevieve, the girl with the yellow plait, said that she wished she were a boy so that she could go too, and she wished she could go anyway, boy or no boy, and as her father said that there was no earthly reason why she should not go, she ran for her hat.

Miss Edith looked as if she would like to go, but she did not say so; and, as for me, I agreed to every proposition. It would certainly be great fun to do things with this lively household.

We started off without the boy, but it was not long before he came running after us, and to my horror I perceived that he carried a rifle.

"What are you going to do with that, Percy?" exclaimed his father.

"I don't expect to do anything with it," the boy replied, "but I thought it would be a good thing to bring it along - especially as Genevieve is with us. Nobody knows what might happen."

"That's true," exclaimed Walter, "and the fact that Genevieve is along is the best reason in the world for your not bringing a gun. You better go take it back."

To this Percy strongly objected. He was going out on a sort of a bear-hunt, and to him half the pleasure would be lost if he did not carry a gun. I am not a coward, but a boy with a gun is a terror to me. My expression may have intimated my state of mind, for Mr. Larramie said to me that we had now gone so far that it would be a pity to send Percy back, and that he did not think there would be any danger, for his boy had been taught how to carry a gun properly.

"We are all out-of-door people and sportsmen," he said, "and we begin early. But I suppose what you are thinking about is the danger of some of us ending soon. But we need not be afraid of that. Walk in front, Percy, and keep the barrel pointed downward."

When we came in sight of the house of the three McKennas, Walter proposed that we make a detour towards the woods. "For," said he, "if those good women see a party like this with a gun among them, they will be sure to think it is a case of escaped criminal, or something of that kind, and be frightened out of their wits."

We skirted the edge of the trees until we came to the opening of the wood road, which I recognized immediately, and, asking Percy and the others to keep back, I went on by myself.

"I don't think people would frighten that sort of a bear," I heard Genevieve say. "He must be used to crowds around him when he's dancing."

I presently reached the place where I had turned from the road. It was a natural break in the woods. There was the tree to which I had tied the bear, but there was no bear.

I stood aghast, and in a moment the rest of the party were clustered around me. "Is this where you left him?" they cried. "And is he gone? Are you sure this is the place?"

Yes, I was sure of it. I have an excellent eye for locality, and I knew that I had chained the bear to the small oak in front of me. At that moment there was a scream from Genevieve. "Look! Look!" she cried. "There he is, just ready to spring!"

We all looked up, and, sure enough, on the lower branch of the oak, half enveloped in foliage, we saw the bear extended at full length and blinking down at us. I gave a shout of delight.

"Now, keep back, all of you!" I cried. "Bears don't spring from trees, but it will be better for you to be out of the way while I try to get him down."

I walked up to the oak-tree, and then I found that the bear was still firmly attached to it. His chain had been fastened loosely around the trunk; he had climbed up to the branch and pulled the chain with him.

I now called upon Orso to come down, but apparently he did not understand English, and lay quietly upon the branch, his head towards the trunk of the tree. I extended my hand up towards the chain, and found that I could nearly reach it. "Shall I give you a lift?" cried Walter, and I accepted the offer. It was a hard piece of work for him, but he was a professed athlete, and he would have lifted me if it had cracked his spine. I reached up and unhooked the chain. It was then long enough for me to stand on the ground and hold the end of it.

Now I began to pull. "Come down!" I said. "Come down, Orso!" But Orso did not move.

"Bears don't come down head-foremost," cried Percy; "they turn around and come down backwards. You ought to have a chain to his tail if you want to pull him down."

"He hasn't got any tail!" exclaimed Genevieve.

I was in a quandary. I might as well try to break the branch as to pull the bear down. "If we had only thought of bringing a bucket of meat!" cried Percy.

"Would you mind holding the chain," I said to Walter,

"while I try to drive him down?" Of course the developed young man was not afraid to do anything I was not afraid to do, and he took the chain. There was a pine-tree growing near the oak, and, mounting into this, I found that with a long stick which Mr. Larramie handed me I could just reach the bear. "Go down!" I said, tapping him on the haunches, but he did not move.

"Can't you speak to him in Italian?" said Genevieve. "Tame bears know Italian. Doesn't anybody know the Italian for 'Come down out of a tree?'" But such knowledge was absent from the party.

"Try him in Latin," cried Percy. "That must be a good deal like Italian, anyway."

To this suggestion Mr. Larramie made no answer; he had left college before any of the party present had been born; Mr. Walter looked a little confused; he had graduated several years before, and his classics were rusty. I felt that my pedagogical position made it incumbent upon me to take immediate action, but for the life of me I could not think of an appropriate phrase.

"Give him high English!" cried Mr. Larramie. "That's often classic enough! Tell him to descend!"

"Orso, descend!" I cried, giving a little foreign twang to the words. Immediately the bear began to twist like a caterpillar upon the limb, he extended his hind-legs towards the trunk, he seized it with his fore-paws. He began slowly to move downward.

"Hurrah!" cried Percy, "that hit him like a rifle-ball! Hurrah for high English! That's good enough for me!"

"Look at his hind hands!" cried Genevieve. "He has worn all

the hair off his palms!"

I hurried from the tree and reached the ground before the bear. Then taking the end of the chain, I advised the others to move out of the woods while I followed with the bear. They all obeyed except Genevieve, who wanted very much to linger behind and help me lead him. But this I would not permit.

The bear followed me with his usual docility until we had emerged from the woods. Then he gave a little start, and fixed his eyes upon Percy, who stood at a short distance, his rifle in his hand. I had not supposed that this bear was afraid of anything, but now I had reason to believe that he was afraid of guns, for the instant he saw the armed boy he made the little start I have mentioned, and followed it up by a great bolt which jerked the chain from my hand, and the next instant Orso was bounding away in great lopes, his chain rattling behind him.

Promptly Percy brought his rifle to his shoulder. "Don't you fire!" I shouted. "Put down your gun and leave it here. It frightens him!" And with that we were all off in hot pursuit.

"Cut him off from the woods!" shouted Mr. Walter, who was in advance. "If he gets in the woods we'll lose him sure!"

We followed this good advice, and at the top of our speed we endeavored to get between the beast and the trees. To a certain extent we succeeded in our object, for some of us were fast runners, and Orso, perceiving that he might be cut off from a woody retreat, turned almost at right angles and made directly for the house.

"He's after the three McKennas!" screamed Genevieve, as she turned to follow the bear, and from being somewhat in the rear she was now in advance of us, and dashed across the field at a most wonderful rate for a girl.

The rest of us soon passed her, but before we reached the house the bear disappeared behind some out-buildings. Then we saw him again. He dashed through the gate of a back yard. He seemed to throw himself against the house. He disappeared through a door-way. There was a great crash as of crockery and tin. There were screams. There was rattling and banging, and then all was still. When we reached the house we heard no sound.

CHAPTER XI

THE THREE McKENNAS

I was in advance, and as I entered the door-way through which the bear had disappeared, I found myself in the kitchen where I had seen the three women at their dinner. Wild confusion had been brought about in a second. A table had been over-turned, broken dishes and tin things were scattered on the floor, a wooden chair lay upon its back, and the room seemed deserted. The rest of the party quickly rushed in behind me, and great were their exclamations at the scene of havoc.

"I hope nothing has happened to the McKenna sisters," cried Mr. Larramie. "They must have been in here!"

I did not suppose that anything serious had occurred, for the bear's jaws were securely strapped, but with anxious haste I went into the other part of the house. Across a hallway I saw an open door, and from the room within came groans, or perhaps I should call them long-drawn wails of woe.

I was in the room in a moment, and the others crowded through the door-way behind me. It was a good-sized bedroom, probably the "spare-room" of the first floor. In one corner was a tall and wide high-posted bedstead, and in the very middle of it sat an elderly woman drawn up into the smallest compass into which she could possibly compress herself. Her eyes were closed, her jaws were dropped, her spectacles hung in front of her mouth, her gray hair straggled over her eyes, and her skin was of a soapy whiteness.

She paid no attention to the crowd of people in the room. Evidently she was frightened out of her senses. Every moment she emitted a doleful wail. As we stood gazing at her, and before we had time to speak to her, she seemed to be seized by an upheaving spasm, the influence of which was so great that she actually rose in the air, and as she did so her wail intensified itself into a shriek, and as she came down again with a sudden thump all the breath in her body seemed to be bounced out in a gasp of woe.

"It's Susan McKenna!" exclaimed Walter. "What in the world is the matter with her? Miss Susan, are you hurt?"

She made no answer, but again she rose, again she gave vent to a wild wail, and again she came down with a thump.

Percy was now on his knees near the bed. "It's the bear!" he cried. "He's under there, and he's humping himself!"

"Sacking bottom!" cried the practical Genevieve "There isn't room enough for him!"

Stooping down I saw the bear under the bed, now crowding himself back as far as possible into a corner. No part of his chain was exposed to view, and for a moment I did not see how I was going to get him out. But the first thing was to get rid of the woman.

"Come, Miss Susan," said Mr. Larramie, "let me help you off the bed, and you can go into another room, and then we will attend to this animal. You need not be afraid to get down. He won't hurt you."

But the McKenna sister paid no attention to these remarks. She kept her eyes closed; she moaned and wailed. So long as that horrible demon was under the bed she would not have put as much as one of her toes over the edge for all the money in the world!

In every way I tried to induce the bear to come out, but he paid no attention to me. He had been frightened, and he was now in darkness and security. Suddenly a happy thought struck me. I glanced around the room, and then I rushed into the hall. Genevieve followed me. "What do you want?" she said.

"I am looking for some overshoes!" I cried. "India-rubber ones!"

Instantly Genevieve began to dash around. In a few moments she had opened a little closet which I had not noticed. "Here is one!" she cried, "but it's torn - the heel is nearly off! Perhaps the other one - "

"Give me that!" I exclaimed. "It doesn't matter about its being torn!" With the old overshoe in my hand I ran back into the room, where Mr. Larramie was still imploring the McKenna sister to get down from the bed. I stooped and thrust the shoe under as far as I could reach. Almost immediately I saw a movement in the shaggy mass in the corner. I wriggled the shoe, and a paw was slightly extended. Then I drew it away slowly from under the bed.

Now, Miss Susan McKenna rose in the air higher than she had yet gone. A maddening wail went up, and for a moment she tottered on the apex of an elevation like a wooden idol upheaved by an earthquake. Before she had time to tumble over she sank again with a thump. The great hairy bear, looking twice as large in that room as he appeared in the open air, came out from under the foot of the bed, and as I dangled the old rubber shoe in front of his nose he would have seized upon it if his jaws had not been strapped together. I got hold of the chain and conducted him quietly outside, amid the cheers and hand-clapping of Percy and Genevieve.

I chained Orso to a post of the fence, and, removing his muzzle, I gave him the old rubber shoe.

"Shall I bring him some more?" cried Genevieve, full of zeal in good works. But I assured her that one would do for the present.

I now hurried into the house to find out what had happened to the persons and property of the McKenna sisters.

"Where are the other two?" cried Genevieve, who was darting from one room to another; "the bear can't have swallowed them."

It was not long before Percy discovered the two missing sisters in the cellar. They were seated on the ground with their aprons over their heads.

It was some time before quiet was restored in that household. To the paralyzing terror occasioned by the sudden advent of the bear succeeded wild lamentations over the loss of property. I assured them that I was perfectly willing to make good the loss, but Mr. Larramie would not allow me to say anything on the subject.

"It is not your affair," said he. "The bear would have done no damage whatever had it not been for the folly of Percy in bringing his gun - I suppose the animal has been shot at some time or other - and my weakness in allowing him to keep it. I will attend to these damages. The amount is very little, I imagine, principally cheap crockery, and the best thing you can do is to start off slowly with your bear. The women will not be able to talk reasonably until it is off the premises. I will catch up with you presently."

When the bear and I, with the rest of the party, were fairly out of sight of the house, we stopped and waited for Mr. Larramie, and it was not long before he joined us.

When we reached the hay-barn we were met by the rest of the Larramie family, all anxious to see the bear. Even Miss Edith, who had had one glimpse of the beast, was very glad indeed to assure me that she did not wonder in the least that I had supposed there would be no harm in leaving such a mild creature for a little while by the side of the road, and I was sure from the exclamations of the rest of the family that Orso would not suffer for want of care and attention during his stay in the hay-barn.

I was immensely relieved to get rid of the bear and to leave him in such good quarters, for it now appeared to me quite reasonable that I might have had difficulty in lodging him anywhere on the premises of the Cheltenham, and under any circumstances I very much preferred appearing at that hotel without an ursine companion. As soon as we reached the house I told Mr. Larramie that it was now necessary for me to hurry on, and asked if there were not some way to the hotel which would not make it necessary for me to go back to the main road.

The good gentleman fairly shouted at me. "You aren't going to any hotel!" he declared. "Do you suppose we are heathens, to let you start off at this late hour in the afternoon for a hotel? You have nothing to do with hotels - you spend the night with us, sir! If you are thinking about your clothes, pray dismiss the subject from your mind. If it will make you feel better satisfied, we will all put on golf suits. In the morning we will get your machine from the Holly Sprig, and when you want to go on we will send you and it to Waterton in a wagon. It is not a long drive, and it is much the pleasanter way to manage your business."

The family showed themselves delighted when they heard that I was to spend the night with them, and I did not object to the plan, for I had not the slightest desire to go to a summer hotel. Just before I went up to my room to get ready for supper, the young Genevieve came to me upon the porch.

"Would you mind," she said, "letting me feel your muscle?"

Very much surprised, I reached out my arm for her inspection, and she clasped her long thin fingers around my *biceps flexor cubiti.* Apparently, the inspection was very satisfactory to her.

"I would give anything," she said, "if I had muscle like that!"

I laughed heartily. "My dear little girl," said I, "you would be sorry, indeed, if you had anything of the sort. When you grow up and go to parties, how would you like to show bare arms shaped like mine? You would be a spectacle, indeed."

"Well," said she, "perhaps you are right. I might not care to have them bulge, but I would like to have them hard."

It was a lively supper and an interesting evening. Miss Edith sat opposite to me at table - I gave her this title because I was informed that there was an elder sister who was away on a visit. I could see that she regarded me as her especial charge. She did not ask me what I would have, but she saw that every possible want was attended to. As the table was lighted by a large hanging-lamp, I had a better view of her features than I had yet obtained. She was not handsome. Her eyes were too wide apart, her nose needed perhaps an eighth of an inch in length, and her well-shaped mouth would not have suffered by a slight reduction. But there was a cheerful honesty in her expression and in her words which gave me the idea that she was a girl to believe in.

After supper we played round games, and the nervous young lady talked. She could not keep her mind on cards, and therefore played no game. In the course of the evening Mrs. Larramie took occasion to say to me, and her eyes were very full as she spoke, that she did not want me to think she had forgotten that that day I had given her her daughter, and although the others - greatly to my satisfaction - did not indulge in any such embarrassing expressions of gratitude, they did not fail to let me know the high estimation in which they held me. The little girl, Clara, sat close to me while I was playing, every now and then gently stroking my arm, and when she was taken off to bed she ran back to say to me that the next time I brought a bear to their house she hoped I would also bring some little ones. Even Percy took occasion to let me know that, under the circumstances, he was willing to overlook entirely the fact of my being a school-master.

After the games, when the family was scattering - not to their several bed-chambers, but apparently to various forms of recreation or study which seemed to demand their attention - Miss Edith asked me if I would not like to take a walk and look at the stars. As this suggestion was made in the presence of her parents, I hesitated a moment, expecting some discreet objection. But none came, and I assented most willingly to a sub-astral promenade.

There was a long, flagged walk which led to the road, and backward and forward upon this path we walked many, many times.

"I like starlight better than moonlight," said Miss Edith, "for it doesn't pretend to be anything more than it is. You cannot do anything by starlight except simply walk about, and if there are any trees, that isn't easy. You know this, you don't expect anything more, and you're satisfied. But moonlight is different. Sometimes it is so bright out-of-doors when the moon is full that you are apt to think you could play golf or croquet, or even sit on a bench and read. But it isn't so. You can't do any of these things - at least, you can't do them with any satisfaction. And yet, month after month, if you live in the country, the moon deceives you into thinking that for a great many things she is nearly as good as the sun. But all she does is to make the world beautiful, and she doesn't do that as well as the sun does it. The stars make no pretences, and that is the reason I like them better.

"But I did not bring you out here to tell you all this," she continued, offering me no opportunity of giving my opinions on the stars and moon. "I simply wanted to say that I am so glad and thankful to be walking about on the surface of the earth with whole bones and not a scratch from head to foot" - at this point my heart began to sink: I never do know what to say when people are grateful to me - "that I am going to show you my gratitude by treating you as I know you would like to be treated. I shall not pour out my gratitude before you and make you say things which are incorrect, for you are bound to do that if you say anything - "

"I thank you from the bottom of my heart," I said; "but now let us talk some more about the stars."

"Oh, bother the stars!" said she. "But I will drop the subject of gratitude as soon as I have said that if you ever come to know me better than you do now, you will know that in regard to such things I am the right kind of a girl."

I had not the slightest doubt that she was entirely correct. And then she began to talk about golf, and after that of croquet.

"I consider that the finest out-door game we have," she said, "because there is more science in it than you find in any of the others. Your brains must work when you play croquet with intelligent opponents."

"The great trouble about it is," I said, "that it is often so easy."

"But you can get rid of that objection," she replied, "if you have a bad ground. Croquet needs hazards just as much as golf does. The finest games I have ever seen were played on a bad ground."

So we talked and walked until some of the lights in the upper windows of the house had gone out. We ascended to the porch, and just before entering the front door she turned to me.

"I wish I could go to sleep to-night with the same right to feel proud, self-confident, superior, that you have. Good-night." And she held out her hand and gave mine a strong, hearty shake.

I smiled as she left me standing on the porch. This was the same spot on which her sister Genevieve had felt my muscle. "This is an appreciative family," I said, and, guided by the sound of voices, I found Mr. Larramie and his son Walter in the billiard-room.

CHAPTER XII

BACK TO THE HOLLY SPRIG

Before going to bed that night I did not throw myself into an easy-chair and gaze musingly out into the night. On the contrary, I stood up sturdily with my back to the mantel-piece, and with the forefinger of my right hand I tapped my left palm.

"Now, then," said I to myself, "as soon as my bicycle is put into working order I shall imitate travellers in hot countries - I shall ride all night, and I shall rest all day. There are too many young women in Cathay. They turn up one after another with the regularity of a continuous performance. No sooner is the curtain rung down on one act than it is rung up on another. Perhaps after a while I may get out of Cathay, and then again I may ride by day."

In taking my things from my valise, I pulled out the little box which the doctor's daughter had given me, but I did not open it. "No," said I, "there is no need whatever that I should take a capsule to-night."

After breakfast the next day Mr. Larramie came to me. "Do you know," said he, "I feel ashamed on account of the plans I made for you."

I did not know, for I could see no earthly reason for such feeling.

"I arranged," said he, "to send to the Holly Sprig for your machine, and then to have you and it driven over to Waterton. Now this I consider brutish. My wife told me that it was, and I agree with her perfectly. It will take several days to repair that injured wheel - Walter tells me you cannot expect it in less than three days - and what will you do in Waterton all that time? It isn't a pretty country, the hotels are barely good enough for a night's stop, and there isn't anything for you to do. Even if you hired a wheel you would find it stupid exploring that country. Now, sir, that plan is brushed entirely out of sight. Your bicycle shall be sent on, and when you hear that it is repaired and ready for use, you can go on yourself if you wish to."

"My dear sir," I exclaimed, "this is entirely too much!"

He put his hands upon my shoulders and looked me squarely in the face. "Too much!" said he, "too much! That may be your opinion, but I can tell you you have the whole of the rest of the world against you. That is, you would have if they all knew the circumstances. Now you are only one, and if you want to know how many people are opposed to you, I have no doubt Percy can tell you, but I am not very well posted in regard to the present population of the world."

There was no good reason that I could offer why I should go and sit solitary in Waterton for three days, and if I had had any such reason I know it would have been treated with contempt. So I submitted - not altogether with an easy mind, and yet seeing cause for nothing but satisfaction and content.

"Another thing," said Mr. Larramie; "I have thought that you would like to attend to your bicycle yourself. Perhaps you will want to take it apart before you send it away. Percy will be glad to drive to the Holly Sprig, and you can go with him. Then, when you come back, I will have my man take your machine to Waterton. I have a young horse very much in need of work, and I shall be glad to have an excuse for giving him some travelling to do." I stood astounded. Go back to the Holly Sprig! This arrangement had been made without reference to me. It had been supposed, of course, that I would be glad to go and attend to the proper packing of my bicycle. Even now, Percy, running across the yard, called to me that he would be ready to start in two minutes.

When I took my seat in the wagon, Mr. Larramie was telling me that he would like me to inform Mrs. Chester that he would keep the bear until it was reasonable to suppose that the owner would not come for it, and that then he would either sell it or buy it himself, and make satisfactory settlement with her.

I know I did not hear all that he said, for my mind was wildly busy trying to decide what I ought to do. Should I jump down even now and decline to go to the Holly Sprig, or should I go on and attend to my business like a sensible man? There was certainly no reason why I should do anything else, but when the impatient Percy started, my mind was not in the least made up; I remained on the seat beside him simply because I was there.

Percy was a good driver, and glad to exhibit his skill. He was also in a lively mood, and talked with great freedom. "Do you know," said he, "that Edith wanted to drive you over to the inn? Think of that! But it had all been cut and dried that I should go, and I was not going to listen to any such nonsense. Besides, you might want somebody to help you take your machine apart and pack it up."

I was well satisfied to be accompanied by the boy and not by his sister, and with the wheels and his tongue rattling along

Frank R. Stockton

together, we soon reached the inn.

Percy drove past it and was about to turn into the entrance of the yard, but I stopped him. "I suppose your wheel is back there," he said.

"Yes," said I, "but I will get out here."

"All right," he replied, "I'll drive around to the sheds."

At the open door of the large room I met Mrs. Chester, evidently on her way out-of-doors. She wore a wide straw hat, her hands were gloved, and she carried a basket and a pair of large shears. When she saw me there was a sudden flush upon her face, but it disappeared quickly. Whether this meant that she was agreeably surprised to see me again, or whether it showed that she resented my turning up again so soon after she thought she was finally rid of me, I did not know. It does not do to predicate too much upon the flushes of women.

I hastened to inform her why I had come, and now, having recovered from her momentary surprise, she asked me to walk in and sit down, an invitation which I willingly accepted, for I did not in the least object to detaining her from her garden.

Now she wanted to know how I had managed to get on with the bear, and what the people at the Cheltenham said about it, and when I went on to tell her the whole story, which I did at considerable length, she was intensely interested. She shuddered at the runaway, she laughed heartily at the uprising of the McKenna sister, and she listened earnestly to everything I had to say about the Larramies.

"You seem to have a wonderful way," she exclaimed, "of falling in with - " I think she was going to say "girls," but she changed it to "people."

"Yes," said I. "I should not have imagined that I could make so many good friends in such a short time."

Then I went on to give her Mr. Larramie's message, and to say more things about the bear. I was glad to think of any subject which might prolong the conversation. So far she was interested, and all that we said seemed perfectly natural to the occasion, but this could not last, and I felt within me a strong desire to make some better use of this interview.

I had not expected to see her again, certainly not so soon, and here I was alone with her, free to say what I chose; but what should I say? I had not premeditated anything serious. In fact, I was not sure that I wished to say anything which should be considered absolutely serious and definite, but if I were ever to do anything definite - and the more I talked with this bright-eyed and merry-hearted young lady the stronger became the longing to say something definite - now was the time to prepare the way for what I might do or say hereafter.

I was beginning to grow nervous, for the right thing to say would not present itself, when Percy strode into the room. "Good-morning, Mrs. Chester," said he, and then, turning to me, he declared that he had been waiting in the yard, and began to think I might have forgotten I had come for my wheel.

Of course I rose and she rose, and we followed Percy to the back door of the house. Outside I saw that the boy of the inn was holding the horse, and that the wheel was already placed in the back part of the wagon.

"I've got everything all right, I think," said Percy. "I didn't suppose it was necessary to wait for you, but you'd better take a look at it to see if you think it will travel without rubbing or damaging itself."

I stepped to the wagon and found that the bicycle was very well placed. "Now, then," said Percy, taking the reins and mounting to his seat, "all you've got to do is to get up, and we'll be off."

I turned to the back door, but she was not there. "Wait a minute," said I, and I hurried into the house. She was not in the hall. I looked into the large room. She was not there. I went into the parlor, and out upon the front porch. Then I went back into the house to seek some one who might call her. I was even willing to avail myself of the services of citric acid, for I could not leave that house without speaking to her again.

In a moment Mrs. Chester appeared from some inner room. I believe she suspected that I had something to say to her which had nothing to do with the bear or the Larramies, for I had been conscious that my speech had been a little rambling, as if I were earnestly thinking of something else than what I was saying, and that she desired I should be taken away without an opportunity to unburden my mind; but now, hearing me tramping about and knowing that I was looking for her, she was obliged to show herself.

As she came forward I noticed that her expression had changed somewhat. There was nothing merry about her eyes; I think she was slightly pale, and her brows were a little contracted, as if she were doing something she did not want to do.

"I hope you found everything all right," she said.

I looked at her steadily. "No," said I, "everything is not all right."

A slight shade of anxiety came upon her face. "I am sorry to hear that," she said. "Was your wheel injured more than you thought?"

"Wheel!" I exclaimed. "I was not thinking of wheels! I will tell you what is not all right! It is not right for me to go away without saying to you that I - "

At this moment there was a strong, shrill whistle from the front of the house. A most unmistakable sense of relief showed itself upon her face. She ran to the front door, and called out, "Yes, he is coming."

There was nothing for me to do but to follow her. I greatly disliked going away without saying what I wanted to say, and I would have been willing to speak even at the front door, but she gave me no chance.

"Good-bye," she said, extending her hand. It was gloved. It gave no clasp - it invited none. As I could not say the words which were on my tongue, I said nothing, and, raising my cap, I hurried away.

To make up for lost time, Percy drove very rapidly. "I came mighty near having a fight while you were in the house," said he. "It was that boy at the inn. He's a queer sort of a fellow, and awfully impertinent. He was talking about you, and he wanted to know if the bear had hurt you. He said he believed you were really afraid of the beast, and only wanted to show off before the women.

"I stood up for you, and I told him about Edith's runaway, and then he said, fair and square, that he didn't believe you stopped the horse. He said he guessed my sister pulled him up herself, and that then you came along and grabbed him and took all the credit. He said he thought you were that sort of a fellow.

"That's the time I was going to pitch into him, but then I thought it would be a pretty low-down thing for me to be fighting a country tavern-boy, so I simply gave him my opinion of him. I don't believe he'd have held the horse, only he thought it would make you get away quicker. He hates you. Did you ever kick him or anything?"

I laughed, and, telling Percy that I had never kicked the boy, I thanked him for his championship of me.

CHAPTER XIII

A MAN WITH A LETTER

When my unfortunate bicycle had been started on its way to Waterton, I threw myself into the family life of the Larramies, determined not to let them see any perturbations of mind which had been caused by the extraordinary promptness of the younger son. If a man had gone with me instead of that boy, I would have had every opportunity of saying what I wanted to say to the mistress of the Holly Sprig. I may state that I frequently found myself trying to determine what it was I wanted to say.

I did my best to suppress all thoughts relating to things outside of this most hospitable and friendly house. I went to see the bear with the younger members of the family. I played four games of tennis, and in the afternoon the whole family went to fish in a very pretty mill-pond about a mile from the house. A good many fish were caught, large and small, and not one of the female fishers, except Miss Willoughby, the nervous young lady, and little Clara, would allow me to take a fish from her hook. Even Mrs. Larramie said that if she fished at all she thought she ought to do everything for herself, and not depend upon other people.

As much as possible I tried to be with Mr. Larramie and Walter. I had not the slightest distaste for the company of the

Frank R. Stockton

ladies, but there was a consciousness upon me that there were pleasant things in which a man ought to restrict himself. There was nothing chronic about this consciousness. It was on duty for this occasion only.

That night at the supper-table the conversation took a peculiar turn. Mr. Larramie was the chief speaker, and it pleased him to hold forth upon the merits of Mrs. Chester. He said, and his wife and others of the company agreed with him, that she was a lady of peculiarly estimable character; that she was out of place; that every one who knew her well felt that she was out of place; but that she so graced her position that she almost raised it to her level. Over and over again her friends had said to her that a lady such as she was - still young, of a good family, well educated, who had travelled, and moved in excellent society - should not continue to be the landlady of a country inn, but the advice of her friends had had no effect upon her.

It was not known whether it was necessary for her to continue the inn-keeping business, but the general belief was that it was not necessary. It was supposed that she had had money when she married Godfrey Chester, and he was not a poor man.

Then came a strange revelation, which Mr. Larramie dwelt upon with considerable earnestness. There was an idea, he said, that Mrs. Chester kept up the Holly Sprig because she thought it would be her husband's wish that she should do so. He had probably said something about its being a provision for her in case of his death. At any rate, she seemed desirous to maintain the establishment exactly as he had ordered it in his life, making no change whatever, very much as if she had expected him to come back, and wished him to find everything as he had left it.

"Of course she doesn't expect him to come back," said Mr.

Larramie, "because it must now be four years since the time of his supposed murder - "

"Supposed!" I cried, with much more excited interest than I would have shown if I had taken proper thought before speaking.

"Well," said Mr. Larramie, "that is a fine point. I said 'supposed' because the facts of the case are not definitely known. There can be no reasonable doubt, however, that he is dead, for even if this fact had not been conclusively proved by the police investigations, it might now be considered proved by his continued absence. It would have been impossible for Mr. Chester alive to keep away from his wife for four years - they were devoted to each other. Furthermore, the exact manner of his death is not known - although it must have been a murder - and for these reasons I used the word 'supposed.' But, really, so far as human judgment can go, the whole matter is a certainty. I have not the slightest doubt in the world that Mrs. Chester so considers it, and yet, as she does not positively know it - as she has not the actual proofs that her husband is no longer living - she refuses in certain ways, in certain ways only, to consider herself a widow."

"And what ways are those?" I asked, in a voice which, I hope, exhibited no undue emotion.

"She declines to marry again," said Mrs. Larramie, now taking up the conversation. "Of course, such a pretty woman - I may say, such a charming woman - would have admirers, and I know that she has had some most excellent offers, but she has always refused to consider any of them. There was one gentleman, a man of wealth and position, who had proposed to her before she married Mr. Chester, who came on here to offer himself again, but she cut off everything he had to say by telling him that as she did not positively know that her husband was not living, she could not allow a word of that sort to be said to her. I know this, because she told me so herself."

There was a good deal more talk of the sort, and of course it interested me greatly, although I tried not to show it, but I could not help wondering why the subject had been brought forward in such an impressive manner upon the present occasion. It seemed to me that there was something personal in it - personal to me. Had that boy Percy been making reports?

In the evening I found out all about it, and in a very straightforward and direct fashion. I discovered Miss Edith by herself, and asked her if all that talk about Mrs. Chester had been intended for my benefit, and, if so, why.

She laughed. "I expected you to come and ask me about that," she said, "for of course you could see through a good deal of it. It is all father's kindness and goodness. Percy was a little out of temper when he came back, and he spun a yarn about your being sweet on Mrs. Chester, and how he could hardly get you away from her, and all that. He had an idea that you wanted to go there and live, at least for the summer. Something a boy said to him made him think that. So father thought that if you had any notions about Mrs. Chester you ought to have the matter placed properly before you without any delay, and I expect his reason for mentioning it at the supper-table was that it might then seem like a general subject of conversation, whereas it would have been very pointed indeed if he had taken you apart and talked to you about it."

"Indeed it would," said I. "And if you will allow me, I will say that boys are unmitigated nuisances! If they are not hearing what they ought not to hear, they are imagining what they ought not to imagine - "

"And telling things that they ought not to tell," she added, with a laugh.

"Which is an extremely bad thing," said I, "when there is nothing to tell."

For the rest of that evening I was more lively than is my wont, for it was a very easy thing to be lively in that family. I do not think I gave any one reason to suppose that I was a man whose attention had been called to a notice not to trespass.

As usual, I communed with myself before going to bed. Wherefore this feeling of disappointment? What did it mean? Would I have said anything of importance, of moment, to Mrs. Chester, if the boy Percy had given me an opportunity? What would I have said? What could I have said? I could see that she did not wish that I should say anything, and now I knew the reason for it. It was all plain enough on her side. Even if she had allowed herself any sort of emotion regarding me, she did not wish me to indulge in anything of the land. But as for myself. I could decide nothing about myself.

I smiled grimly as my eyes fell upon the little box of capsules. My first thought was that I should take two of them, but then I shook my head. "It would be utterly useless," I said; "they would do me no good."

In the course of the next morning I found myself alone. I put on my cap, lighted a pipe, and started down the flag walk to the gate. In a few moments I heard running steps behind me, and, turning, I saw Miss Edith. "Don't look cross," she said. "Were you going for a walk?"

I scouted the idea of crossness, and said that I had thought of taking a stroll.

"That seems funny," said she, "for nobody in this house ever goes out for a lonely walk. But you cannot go just yet. There's a man at the back of the house with a letter for you."

"A letter!" I exclaimed. "Who in the world could have sent a letter to me here?"

"The only way to find out," she answered, "is to go and see."

Under a tree at the back of the house I found a young negro man, very warm and dusty, who handed me a letter, which, to my surprise, bore no address. "How do you know this is for me?" said I.

He was a good-natured looking fellow. "Oh, I know it's for you, sir," said he. "They told me at the little tavern - the Holly something - that I'd find you here. You're the gentle-man that had a bicycle tire eat up by a bear, ain't you?"

I admitted that I was, and still, without opening the letter, I asked him, where it came from.

"That was given to me in New York, sir," said he, "by a Dago, one of these I-talians. He gave me the money to go to Blackburn Station in the cars, and then I walked over to the tavern. He said he thought I'd find you there, sir. He told me just what sort of a lookin' man you was, sir, and that letter is for you, and no mistake. He didn't know your name, or he'd put it on."

"Oh, it is from the owner of the bear," said I.

"Yes, sir," said the man, "that's him. He did own a bear - he told me - that eat up your tire."

I now tore open the blank envelope, and found it contained a letter on a single sheet, and in this was a folded paper, very dirty. The letter was apparently written in Italian, and had no signature. I ran my eye along the opening lines, and soon found that it would be a very difficult piece of business for me to read it. I was a fair French and German scholar, but my knowledge of Italian was due entirely to its relationship with Latin. I told the man to rest himself somewhere, and went to the house, and, finding Miss Edith, I informed her that I had a letter from the bear man, and asked her if she could read Italian.

"I studied the language at school," she said, "but I have not practised much. However, let us go into the library - there is a dictionary there - and perhaps we can spell it out."

We spread the open sheet upon the library-table, and laid the folded paper near by, and, sitting side by side, with a dictionary before us, we went to work. It was very hard work.

"I think," said my companion, after ten minutes' application, "that the man who sent you this letter writes Italian about as badly as we read it. I think I could decipher the meaning of his words if I knew what letters those funny scratches were intended to represent. But let us stick to it. After a while we may get a little used to the writing, and I must admit that I have a curiosity to know what the man has to say about his bear."

After a time the work became easier. Miss Edith possessed an acuteness of perception which enabled her to decipher almost illegible words by comparing them with others which were better written. We were at last enabled to translate the letter. The substance of it was as follows:

The writer came to New York on a ship. There was a man on the ship, an Italian man, who was very wicked. He did very wicked things to the writer. When he got to New York he

Frank R. Stockton

kept on being wicked. He was so wicked that the writer made up his mind to kill him. He waited for him one night for two hours.

At last the moment came. It was very dark, and the victim came, walking fast. The avenger sprang from a door-way and plunged his knife into the back of the victim. The man fell, and the moment he fell the writer of the letter knew that he was not the man he had intended to kill. The wicked man would not have been killed so easily. He turned over the man. He was dead. His eyes were used to the darkness, and he could see that he was the wrong man.

The coat of the murdered man had fallen open, and a paper showed itself in an inside pocket. The Italian waited only long enough to snatch this paper. He wanted to have something which had belonged to that poor, wrongly murdered man. After that he heard no more about the great mistake he had committed. He could not read the newspapers, and he asked nobody any questions. He put the paper away and kept it. He often thought he ought to burn the paper, but he did not do it. He was afraid. The paper had a name on it, and he was sure it was the name of the man he had killed. He thought as long as he kept the paper there was a chance for his forgiveness.

This was all four years ago. He worked hard, and after a while he bought a bear. When his bear ate up the India-rubber on my bicycle he was very much frightened, for he was afraid he might be sent to prison. But that was not the fright that made him run away.

When he talked to the boy and asked him the name of the keeper of the inn, and the boy told him what it was, the earth seemed to open and he saw hell. The name was the name that was on the paper he had taken from the man he had killed by mistake, and this was his wife whose house he was staying at. He was seized with such a horror and such a fear that everything might be found out, and that he would be arrested, that he ran away to the railroad and took a train for New York.

He did not want his bear. He did not want to be known as the man who had been going about with a bear. One thing he wanted, and that was to get back to Italy, where he would be safe. He was going back very soon in a ship. He had changed his name. He could not be found any more. But he knew his soul would never have any peace if he did not send the paper to the wife of the man he had made a mistake about. But he could not write a letter to her, so he sent it to me, for me to give her the paper and to tell her what he had written in the letter. He left America forever. Nobody in this country would ever see him again. He was gone. He was lost to all people in this country, but his soul felt better now that he had done that which would make the lady whose husband he had killed know how it had happened. The bear he would give to her. That was all that he could do for her.

There was no formal close to the letter; the writer had said what he had to say and stopped.

Miss Edith and I looked at each other. Her eyes had grown large and bright. "Now, shall we examine the paper?"

"I do not know that we have a right to do so," I said. I know my voice was trembling, for I was very much agitated. "That belongs to - to her!"

"I think," said Miss Edith, "that we ought to look at it. It is merely a folded paper. I do not think we ought to thrust information upon Mrs. Chester without knowing what it is. Perhaps the man made a mistake in the name. We may do a great deal of mischief if we do not know exactly what we are about." And so saying she took the paper and opened it.

Frank R. Stockton

It was nothing but a grocery bill, but it was made out to - Godfrey Chester, Dr. Evidently it was for goods supplied to the inn. It was receipted.

For a few moments I said nothing, and then I exclaimed, in tones which made my companion gaze very earnestly at me: "I must go to her immediately! I must take these papers! She must know everything!"

"Excuse me," said Miss Edith, "but don't you think that something ought to be done about apprehending this man - this Italian? Let us go and question his messenger." We went out together, she carrying, tightly clasped, both the letter and the bill.

The black man could tell us very little. An Italian he had never seen before had given him the letter to take to Holly Sprig Inn, and give to the gentleman who had had his tire eaten by a bear. If the gentleman was not there, he was to ask to have it sent to him. That was everything he knew.

"Did the Italian give you money to go back with?" asked Miss Edith, and the man rather reluctantly admitted that he did.

"Well, you can keep that for yourself," said she, "and we'll pay your passage back. But we would like you to wait here for a while. There may be some sort of an answer."

The man laughed. "'Taint no use sendin' no answer," said he; "I couldn't find that Dago again. They're all so much alike. He said he was goin' away on a ship. You see it was yesterday he gave me that letter. I 'spect he'll be a long way out to sea before I get back, even if I did know who he was and what ship he was goin' on. But if you want me to wait, I don't mind waitin'."

"Very good," said Miss Edith; "you can go into the kitchen and have something to eat." And, calling a maid, she gave orders for the man's entertainment.

"Now," said she, turning to me, "let us take a walk through the orchard. I want to talk to you."

"No," said I, "I can't talk at present. I must go immediately to the inn with those papers. It is right that not a moment should be lost in delivering this most momentous message which has been intrusted to me."

"But I must speak to you first," said she, and she walked rapidly towards the orchard. As she still held the papers in her hand, I was obliged to follow her.

CHAPTER XIV

MISS EDITH IS DISAPPOINTED

As soon as we had begun to walk under the apple-trees she turned to me and said: "I don't think you ought to take this letter and the bill to Mrs. Chester. It would not be right. There would be something cruel about it."

"What do you mean?" I exclaimed.

"Of course I do not know exactly the state of the case," she answered, "but I will tell you what I think about it as far as I know. You must not be offended at what I say. If I am a friend to anybody - and I would be ashamed if I were not a friend to you - I must tell him just what I think about things, and this is what I think about this thing: I ought to take these papers to Mrs. Chester. I know her well enough, and it is a woman who ought to go to her at such a time."

"That message was intrusted to me," I said. "Of course it was," she answered, "but the bear man did not know what he was doing. He did not understand the circumstances."

"What circumstances?" I asked.

She gave me a look as if she were going to take aim at me and wanted to be sure of my position. Then she said: "Percy told us he thought you were courting Mrs. Chester. That was pure impertinence on his part, and perhaps what father said at the table was impertinence too, but I know he said it because he thought there might be something in Percy's chatter, and that you ought to understand how things stood. Now, you may think it impertinence on my part if you choose, but it really does seem to me that you are very much interested in Mrs. Chester. Didn't you intend to walk down to the Holly Sprig when you were starting out by yourself this morning?"

"Yes," said I, "I did."

"I thought so," she replied. "That, of course, was your own business, and what father said about her being unwilling to marry again need not have made any difference to you if you had chosen not to mind it. But now, don't you think, if you look at the matter fairly and squarely, it would be pretty hard on Mrs. Chester if you were to go down to her and make her understand that she really is a widow, and that now she is free to listen to you if you want to say anything to her? This may sound a little hard and cruel, but don't you think it is the way she would have to look at it?"

She stopped as she spoke, and I turned and stood silent, looking at her.

"My first thought was," she said, "to advise you to tell father about all this, and take his advice about telling her, but I don't think you would like that. Now, would you like that?"

"No," I answered, "I certainly would not."

"And don't you really think I ought to go to her with the message, and then come back and tell you how she took it and what she said?"

For nearly a minute I did not speak, but I knew she was right, and at last I admitted it.

"I am glad to hear you say so!" she exclaimed. "As soon as dinner is over I shall drive to the Holly Sprig."

We still walked on, and she proposed that we should go to the top of a hill beyond the orchard, where there was a pretty view.

"You may think me a strange sort of a girl," she said, presently, "but I can't help it. I suppose I am strange. I have often thought I would like very much to talk freely and honestly with a man about the reasons which people have for falling in love with each other. Of course I could not ask my father or brother, because they would simply laugh at me and tell me that falling in love was very much like the springing up of weeds - generally without reason and often objectionable. But you would be more likely to tell me something which would be of advantage to me in my studies."

"Your studies!" I exclaimed. "What in the world are you studying?"

"Well, I am studying human nature - not as a whole, of course, that's too large a subject, but certain phases of it - and I particularly want to know why such queer people come together and get married. Now I have great advantages in such a study, much greater than most girls have."

"What are they?" I asked.

"The principal one is that I never intend to marry. I made up my mind to that a good while ago. There is a great deal of work that I want to do in this world, and I could not do it properly if I were tied to a man. I would either have to submit myself to his ways, or he would have to submit himself to my ways, and that would not suit me. In the one case I should not respect him, and in the other I should not respect myself."

"But suppose," said I, "you should meet a man who should be in perfect harmony with you in all important points?"

"Ah," she said, "that sort of thing never happens. You might as well expect to pick up two pebbles exactly alike. I don't believe in it. But if at any time during the rest of my life you show me any examples of such harmony, I will change my opinions. I believe that if I can wait long enough, society will catch up with me. Everything looks that way to me."

"It may be that you are right," I answered. "Society is getting on famously. But what is it you want to ask me?"

"Simply this," she replied. "What is it which interests you so much in Mrs. Chester?"

I looked at her in astonishment. "Truly," I exclaimed, "that is a remarkable question."

"I know it," she replied, "and I suppose you are saying to yourself, 'Here is a girl who has known me less than three days, and yet she asks me to tell her about my feeling towards another woman.' But, really, it seems to me that as you have not known that other woman three days, as much friendship and confidence might spring up in the one case as affection in the other."

"Affection!" said I. "Have I said anything about affection?"

"No, you have not," she replied; "and if there isn't any affection, of course that ends this special study on my part."

We reached the top of the hill, but I forgot to look out upon the view. "I think you are a strange girl," I said, "but I like you, and I have a mind to try to answer your question. I have not been able quite to satisfy myself about my feelings towards Mrs. Chester, but now I think I can say that I have an affection for her."

"Good!" she exclaimed. "I like that! That is an honest answer if ever there was one. But tell me why it is that you have an affection for her. It must have been almost a case of love at first sight."

"It isn't easy to give reasons for such feelings," I said. "They spring up, as your father would say, very much like weeds."

"Indeed they do," she interpolated; "sometimes they grow in the middle of a gravel path where they cannot expect to be allowed to stay."

I reflected a moment. "I don't mind talking about these things to you," I said. "It seems almost like talking to myself."

"That is a compliment I appreciate," she said. "And now go on. Why do you care for her?"

"Well," said I, "in the first place, she is very handsome. Don't you think so?"

"Oh yes! In fact, I think she is almost what might be called exactly beautiful."

"Then she has such charming manners," I continued. "And she is so sensible - although you may not think I had much chance to find out that. Moreover, there is a certain sympathetic cordiality about her - "

"Which, of course," interrupted my companion, "you suppose she would not show to any man but you."

"Yes," said I. "I am speaking honestly now, and that's the way it strikes me. Of course I may be a fool, but I did think that a sympathy had arisen between us which would not arise between her and anybody else."

Miss Edith laughed heartily. "I am getting to know a great deal about one side of the subject," she said. "And now tell me - is that all? I don't believe it is."

"No," I answered, "it is not. There is something more which makes her attractive to me. I cannot exactly explain it except by saying that it is her surrounding atmosphere - it is everything that pertains to her. It is the life she lives, it is her home, it is the beauty and peace, the sense of charm which infuses her and everything that belongs to her."

"Beautiful!" said Miss Edith. "I expected an answer like that, but not so well put. Now let me translate it into plain, simple language. What you want is to give up your present life, which must be awfully stupid, and go and help Mrs. Chester keep the Holly Sprig. That would suit you exactly. A charming wife, charming surroundings, charming sense of living, a life of absolute independence! But don't think," she added, quickly, "that I am imputing any sordid motives to you. I meant nothing of the kind. You would do just as much to make the inn popular as she would. I expect you would make her rich."

"Miss Edith Larramie," said I, "you are a heartless deceiver! It makes my blood run cold to hear you speak in that way."

"Never mind that," she said, "but tell me, didn't you think it would be just lovely to live with her in that delightful little inn?"

I could not help smiling at her earnestness, but I answered that I did think so.

Frank R. Stockton

She nodded her head reflectively. "Yes," she said, "I was right. I think you ought to admit that I am a good judge of human nature - at least, in some people and under certain circumstances."

"You are," said I. "I admit that. Now answer me a question. What do you think of it?"

"I don't like it," she said. "And don't you see," she added, with animation, "what an advantage I possess in having determined never to marry? Very few other girls would be willing to speak to you so plainly. They would be afraid you would think that they wanted you, but, as I don't want anybody, you and I can talk over things of this kind like free and equal human beings. So I will say again that I don't like your affection for Mrs. Chester. It disappoints me."

"Disappoints you!" I exclaimed.

"Yes," she said, "that is the word. You must remember that my acquaintance with you began with a sort of a bump. A great deal happened in an instant. I formed high ideas of you, and among them were ideas of the future. You can't help that when you are thinking of people who interest you. Your mind will run ahead. When I found out about Mrs. Chester I was disappointed. It might be all very delightful, but you ought to do better than that!"

"How old are you?" I asked.

"Twenty-two last May," she replied.

"Isn't that the dinner-bell I hear in the distance?" I said.

"Yes," she answered, "and we will go down."

On the way she stopped, and we stood facing each other. "I

am greatly obliged to you," she said, "for giving me your confidence in this way, and I want you to believe that I shall be thoroughly loyal to you, and that I never will breathe anything you have said. But I also want you to know that I do not change any of my opinions. Now we understand each other, don't we?"

"Yes," I answered, "but I think I understand you better than you understand me."

"Not a bit of it," she replied; "that's nonsense. Do you see that flower-pot on the top of the stump by the little hill over there? Percy has been firing at it with his air-gun. Do you think you could hit it with an apple? Let's each take three apples and try."

It was late in the afternoon when Miss Edith returned from the Holly Sprig, where she and Genevieve had driven in a pony-cart. I was with the rest of the family on the golf links a short distance from the house, and it was some time before she got a chance to speak to me, but she managed at last.

"How did she take the news?" I eagerly asked.

The girl hesitated. "I don't think I ought to tell you all she said and did. It was really a private interview between us two, and I know she would not want me to say much about it. And I don't think you would want to hear everything."

I hastened to assure her that I would not ask for the particulars of the conversation. I only wished to know the general effect of the message upon her. That was legitimate enough, as, in fact, she received the message through me.

"Well, she was very much affected, and it would have teen dreadful if you had gone. Oh the whole, however, I cannot help thinking that the Italian's letter was a great relief to her, particularly because she found that her husband had been killed by mistake. She said that one of the greatest loads upon her soul had been the feeling that he had had an enemy who hated him enough to kill him. But now the case is very different, and it is a great comfort to her to know it."

"And about the murderer?" I said. "Did you ask her if she wanted steps taken to apprehend him?"

"Yes," she said, "I did speak of it, and she is very anxious that nothing shall be done in that direction. Even if the Italian should be caught, she would not have the affair again publicly discussed and dissected. She believes the man's story, and she never wants to hear of him again. Indeed, I think that if it should be proved that the Italian killed Mr. Chester on purpose, it would be the greatest blow that could be inflicted upon her."

"Then," said I, "I might as well let the negro man go his way. I have not paid him his passage-money to the city. I knew he would wait until he got it, and it might be desirable to take him into custody."

"Oh no," she said. "Mrs. Chester spoke about that. She doesn't want the man troubled in any way. He knew nothing of the message he carried. Now I am going to tell father about it - she asked me to do it."

That evening was a merry one. We had charades, and a good many other things were going on. Miss Willoughby was an admirable actress, and Miss Edith was not bad, although she could never get rid of her personality. I was in a singular state of mind. I felt as if I had been relieved from a weight. My spirits were actually buoyant.

"You should not be so unreasonably gay," said Miss Edith to me. "That may be your way when you get better acquainted with people, but I am afraid some of the family will think that you are in such good spirits because Mrs. Chester now knows that she is a widow."

"Oh, there is no danger of their thinking anything of that sort," I said. "Don't you suppose they will attribute my good spirits to the fact that the man who took my bicycle to Waterton brought back my big valise, so that I am enabled to look like a gentleman in the parlor? And then, as he also brought word that my bicycle will be all ready for me to-morrow, don't you think it is to be expected of me that I should try to make myself as agreeable as possible on this my last evening with all you good friends?"

She shook her head. "Those excuses will not pass. You are abnormally cheerful. My study of you is extremely interesting, but not altogether satisfactory."

CHAPTER XV

MISS WILLOUGHBY

It was decreed the next day that I should not leave until after dinner. They would send me over to Blackburn Station by a cross-road, and I could then reach Waterton in less than an hour. "There is another good thing about this arrangement," said Miss Edith, for it was she who announced it to me, "and that is that you can take charge of Amy."

I gazed at her mystified, and she said, "Don't you know that Miss Willoughby is going in the same train with you?"

"What!" I exclaimed, far too forcibly.

"Yes. Her visit ends to-day. She lives in Waterton. But why should that affect you so wonderfully? I am sure you cannot object to an hour in the train with Amy Willoughby. She may talk a good deal, but you must admit that she talks well."

"Object!" I said. "Of course I don't object. She talks very well indeed, and I shall be glad to have the pleasure of her company."

"No one would have thought so," she said, looking at me with a criticising eye, "who had seen you when you heard she was going."

"It was the suddenness," I said.

"Oh yes," she replied, "and your delicate nerves."

In my soul I cried out to myself: "Am I ever to break free from young women! Is there to be a railroad accident between here and Waterton! If so, I shall save the nearest old gentleman!"

I believe the Larramies were truly sorry to have me go. Each one of them in turn told me so. Mrs. Larramie again said to me, with tears in her eyes, that it made her shudder to think what that home might be if it had not been for me.

Mr. Larramie and Walter promised to get up some fine excursions if I would stay a little longer, and Genevieve made me sit down beside her under a tree.

"I am awfully sorry you are going," she said. "I always wanted a gentleman friend, and I believe if you'd stay a little longer you'd be one. You see, Walter is really too old for me to confide in, and Percy thinks he's too old - and that's a great deal worse. But you're just the age I like. There are so many things I would say to you if you lived here."

Little Clara, cried when she heard I was going, and I felt myself obliged to commit the shameful deception of talking about baby bears and my possible return to this place.

Miss Edith accompanied us to the station, and when I took leave of her on the platform she gave me a good, hearty handshake. "I believe that we shall see each other again," she said, "and when we meet I want you to make a report, and I hope it will be a good one!"

"About what?" I asked.

She smiled in gentle derision, and the conductor cried, "All aboard!"

I found a vacant seat, and, side by side, Miss Willoughby and I sped on towards Waterton.

For some time I had noticed that Miss Willoughby had ceased to look past me when she spoke to me, and now she fixed her eyes fully upon me and said:

"I am always sorry when I go away from that house, for I think the people who live there are the dearest in the world, excepting my own mother and aunt, who are nearer to me than anybody else, although, if I needed a mother, Mrs. Larramie would take me to her heart, I am sure, just as if I were her own daughter, and I am not related to them in any way, although I have always looked upon Edith as a sister, and I don't believe that if I had a real sister she could possibly have been as dear a girl as Edith, who is so lovable and tender and forgiving - whenever there is anything to forgive - and who, although she is a girl of such strong character and such a very peculiar way of thinking about things, has never said a hard word to me in all her life, even when she found that our opinions were different, which was something she often did find, for she looks upon everything in this world in her own way, and bases all her judgments upon her own observations and convictions, while I am very willing to let those whom I think I ought to look up to and respect judge for me - at least in a great many things, but of course not in all matters, for there are some things which we must decide for ourselves without reference to other people's opinions, though I should be sorry indeed if I had so many things to decide as Edith has, or rather chooses to have, for if she would depend more upon other people I think it would not only be easier for her, but really make her happier, for if you could hear some of the wonderful things which she has discussed with me after we have gone to bed at night it would really make your head ache - that is, if you are subject to that sort of thing, which I am if I am kept awake too long, but I am proud to say that I don't think I ever allowed Edith to suppose that I was tired of hearing her talk, for when any one is as lovely as she is I think she ought to be allowed to talk about what she pleases and just along as she pleases."

Surprising as it may appear, nothing happened on that railroad journey. No cow of Cathay blundered in front of the locomotive; no freight train came around a curve going in the opposite direction upon the same track; everything went smoothly and according to schedule. Miss Willoughby did not talk all the time. She was not the greatest talker I ever knew; she was not even the fastest; she was always willing to wait until her turn came, but she had wonderful endurance for a steady stretch. She never made a bad start, she never broke, she went steadily over the track until the heat had been run.

When the time came for me to speak she listened with great interest, and sometimes at my words her eyes sparkled almost as much as they did when she was speaking herself. She knew a great many things, and I was pleased to find out that she was especially interested in the good qualities of the people she knew. I never heard so many gracious sentiments in so short a time.

Miss Willoughby's residence was but a short distance from the station at Waterton; and as she thought it entirely unnecessary to take a cab, I attended to her baggage, and offered to walk with her to her home and carry her little bag. I was about to leave her at the door, but this she positively forbade. I must step in for a minute or two to see her mother and her aunt They had heard of me, and would never forgive her if she let me go without their seeing me. As the door opened immediately, we went in.

Miss Willoughby's mother and aunt were two most charming elderly ladies, immaculately dainty in their dress, cordial of manner, bright of eye, and diminutive of hand, producing the impression of gentle goodness set off by soft white muslin, folded tenderly.

They had heard of me. In the few days in which I had been with the Larramies, Miss Willoughby had written of me. They insisted that I should stay to supper, for what good reason could there be for my taking that meal at the hotel - not a very good one - when they would be so glad to have me sup with them and talk about our mutual friends?

I had no reasonable objection to offer, and, returning to the station, I took my baggage to the hotel, where I prepared to sup with the Willoughby family.

They were now a little family of three, although there was a brother who had started away the day before on a bicycling tour very like my own, and they were both so delighted to have Amy visit the Larramies, and they were both so delighted to have her come back.

The supper was a delicate one, suitable for canary birds, but at an early stage of the meal a savory little sirloin steak was brought on which had been cooked especially for me. Of course I could not be expected to be satisfied with thin dainties, no matter how tasteful they might be.

This house was the abode of intelligence, cultivated taste, and opulence. It was probably the finest mansion of the town. In every room there were things to see, and after supper we looked at them, and, as I wandered from pictures to vases and carved ivory, the remarks of the two elder ladies and Miss Willoughby seemed like a harmonized chorus accompanying the rest of the performance. Each spoke at the right time, each in her turn said the thing she ought to say. It was a rare exhibition of hospitable enthusiasm, tempered by sympathetic consideration for me and for each other.

I soon discovered that many of the water-color drawings on the walls were the work of Miss Willoughby, and when she saw I was interested in them she produced a portfolio of her sketches. I liked her coloring very much. It was sometimes better than her drawing. It was dainty, delicate, and suggestive. One picture attracted me the moment my eyes fell upon it; it was one of the most carefully executed, and it represented the Holly Sprig Inn.

"You recognize that!" said Miss Willoughby, evidently pleased. "You see that light-colored spot in the portico? That's Mrs. Chester; she stood there when I was making the drawing. It is nothing but two or three little dabs, but that is the way she looked at a distance. Around on this side is the corner of the yard where the bear tried to eat up the tire of your bicycle."

I gazed and gazed at the little light-colored spot in the portico. I gave it form, light, feeling. I could see perfect features, blue eyes which looked out at me, a form of simple grace.

I held that picture a good while, saying little, and scarcely listening to Miss Willoughby's words. At last I felt obliged to replace it in the portfolio. If the artist had been a poor girl, I would have offered to buy it; if I had known her better, I would have asked her to give it to me; but I could do nothing but put it back.

Glancing at the clock I saw that it was time for me to go, but when I announced this fact the ladies very much demurred. Why should I go to that uncomfortable hotel? They would send for my baggage. There was not the least reason in the world why I should spend the night in that second-rate establishment.

"See," said Mrs. Willoughby, opening the door of a room in the rear of the parlor, "if you will stay with us to-night we will lodge you in the chamber of the favored guest. All the pictures on the walls were done by my daughter."

I looked into the room. It was the most charming and luxurious bedroom I had ever seen. It was lighted, and the harmony of its furnishings was a treat to the eye.

But I stood firm in my purpose to depart. I would not spend the night in that house. There would be a fire, burglars, I knew not what! Against all kind entreaties I urged the absolute necessity of my starting away by the very break of day, and I could not disturb a private family by any such proceeding. They saw that I was determined to go, and they allowed me to depart.

CHAPTER XVI

AN ICICLE

My room at the hotel was as dreary as a stubble-field upon a November evening. The whole house was new, varnished, and hard. My bedroom was small. A piece of new ingrain carpet covered part of the hard varnished floor. Four hard walls and a ceiling, deadly white, surrounded me. The hard varnished bedstead (the mattress felt as if it were varnished) nearly filled the little room. Two stiff chairs, and a yellow window-shade which looked as if it were made of varnished wood, glittered in the feeble light of a glass lamp, while the ghastly grayish pallor of the ewer and basin on the wash-stand was thrown into bold relief by the intenser whiteness of the wall behind it.

I put out my light as soon as possible and resolutely closed my eyes, for a street lamp opposite my window would not allow the room to fade into obscurity, and, as long as the hardness of the bed prevented me from sleeping, my thoughts ran back to the chamber of the favored guest, but my conscience stood by me. Cathay is a country where it is necessary to be very careful.

I did not leave Waterton until after nine o'clock the next day, for, although I was early at the shop to which my bicycle had been sent, it was not quite ready for me, and I had to wait.

Frank R. Stockton

Fortunately no Willoughby came that way.

But when at last I mounted my wheel I sped away rapidly towards the north. I had ordered my baggage expressed to a town fifty miles away, and I hoped that if I rode steadily and kept my eyes straight in front of me I might safely get out of Cathay, for the boundaries of that fateful territory could not extend themselves indefinitely.

Towards the close of the afternoon I saw a female in front of me, her back to me, walking, and pushing a bicycle.

"Now," said I to myself, "she is doing that because she likes it, and it is none of my business." I gazed over the fields on the other side of the road, but as I passed her I could not help giving a glance at her machine. The air was gone from the tire of the hind wheel.

"Ah," said I to myself, "perhaps her pump is out of order, or it may be that she does not know how to work it. It is getting late. She may have to go a long distance. I could pump it up for her in no time. Even if there is a hole in it I could mend it." But I did not stop. I had steeled my heart against any more adventures in Cathay.

But my conscience did not stand by me. I could not forget that poor woman plodding along the weary road and darkness not far away. I went slower and slower, and at last I turned.

"It would not take me five minutes to help her," I said. "I must be careful, but I need not be a churl." And I rode rapidly back.

I came in sight of her just as she was turning into the gateway of a pretty house yard. Doubtless she lived there. I turned again and spun away faster than I had gone that day.

For more than a month I journeyed and sojourned in a beautiful river valley and among the low foot-hills of the mountains. The weather was fair, the scenery was pleasing, and at last I came to believe that I had passed the boundaries of Cathay. I took no tablets from my little box. I did not feel that I had need of them.

In the course of time I ceased to travel north-ward. My vacation was not very near its end, but I chose to turn my face towards the scene of my coming duties. I made a wide circuit, I rode slowly, and I stopped often.

One day I passed through a village, and at the outer edge of it a little girl, about four years old, tried to cross the road. Tripping, she fell down almost in front of me. It was only by a powerful and sudden exertion that I prevented myself from going over her, and as I wheeled across the road my machine came within two feet of her. She lay there yelling in the dust. I dismounted, and, picking her up I carried her to the other side of the road. There I left her to toddle homeward while I went on my way. I could not but sigh as I thought that I was again in Cathay.

Two days after this I entered Waterton. There was another road, said to be a very pleasant one, which lay to the west-ward, and which would have taken me to Walford through a country new to me, but I wished to make no further explorations in Cathay, and if one journeys back upon a road by which he came he will find the scenery very different.

I spent the night at the hotel, and after breakfast I very reluctantly went to call upon the Willoughbys. I forced myself to do this, for, considering the cordiality they had shown me, it would have required more incivility than I possessed to pass through the town without paying my respects. But to my great joy none of the ladies was at home. I hastened from the house with a buoyant step, and was soon

Frank R. Stockton

speeding away, and away, and away.

The road was dry and hard, the sun was bright, but there was a fresh breeze in my face, and I rolled along at a swift and steady rate. On, on I went, until, before the sun had reached its highest point, I wheeled out of the main road, rolled up a gravel path, and dismounted in front of the Holly Sprig Inn.

I leaned my bicycle against a tree and went in-doors. The place did not seem so quiet as when I first saw it. I had noticed a lady sitting under a tree in front of the house. There was a nurse-maid attending a child who was playing on the grass. Entering the hall, I glanced into the large room which I had called the "office," and saw a man there writing at a table.

Presently a maid-servant came into the hall. She was not one I had noticed before. I asked if I could see Mrs. Chester, and she said she would go and look for her. There were chairs in the hall, and I might have waited for her there, but I did not. I entered the parlor, and was pleased to find it unoccupied. I went to the upper end of the room, as far as possible from the door.

In a few minutes I heard a step in the hall. I knew it, and it was strange how soon I had learned to know it. She stopped in front of the office, then she went on towards the porch, and turning she came into the parlor, first looking towards the front of the room and then towards the place where I stood.

The light from a window near me fell directly upon her as she approached me, and I could see that there was a slight flush on her face, but before she reached me it had disappeared. She did not greet me. She did not offer me her hand. In fact, from what afterwards happened, I believe that she did not consider me at that moment a fit subject for ordinary greeting. She stood up in front of me. She gazed steadfastly into my face. Her features wore something of their ordinary pleasant expression, but to this there was added a certain determination which I had never seen there before. She gave her head a little quick shake.

"No, sir!" she said.

This reception amazed me. I had been greatly agitated as I heard her approach, turning over in my mind what I should first say to her, but now I forgot everything I had prepared. "No what?" I exclaimed.

"'No' means that I will not marry you."

I stood speechless. "Of course you are thinking," she continued, "that you have never asked me to marry you. But that isn't at all necessary. As soon as I saw you standing there, back two weeks before your vacation is over, and when I got a good look at your face, I knew exactly what you had come for. I was afraid when you left here that you would come back for that, so I was not altogether unprepared. I spoke promptly so as to spare you and to make it easier for me."

"Easier!" I repeated. "What do you mean?"

"Easier, because the sooner you know that I will not marry you the better it will be for you and for me."

Now I could restrain myself no longer. "Why can't I marry you?" I asked, speaking very rapidly, and, I am afraid, with imprudent energy. "Is it any sort of condition or circumstance which prevents? Do you think that I am forcing myself upon you at a time when I ought not to do it? If so, you have mistaken me. Ever since I left here I have thought of scarcely anything but you, and I have returned thus early simply to tell you that I love you! I had to do that! I could not wait! But as to all else, I can wait, and wait, and wait, as long as you please. You can tell me to go away and come back at whatever time you think it will be right for you to give me an answer."

"This is the right time," she said, "and I have given you your answer. But, unfortunately, I did not prevent you from saying what you came to say. So now I will tell you that the conditions and circumstances to which you allude have nothing to do with the matter. I have a reason for my decision which is of so much more importance than any other reason that it is the only one which need be considered."

"What is that?" I asked, quickly.

"It is because I keep a tavern," she answered. "It would be wrong and wicked for you to marry a woman who keeps a tavern."

Now my face flushed. I could feel it burning. "Keep a tavern!" I exclaimed. "That is a horrible way to put it! But why should you think for an instant that I cared for that? Do you suppose I consider that a dishonorable calling? I would be only too glad to adopt it myself and help you keep a tavern, as you call it."

"That is the trouble!" she exclaimed. "That is the greatest trouble. I believe you would. I believe that you think that the life would just suit you."

"Then sweep away the tavern!" I exclaimed. "Banish it. Leave it. Put it out of all thought or consideration. I can wait for you. I can make a place and a position for you. I can - "

"No, you cannot," she interrupted. "At least, not for a long time, unless one of your scholars dies and leaves you a legacy. It is the future that I am thinking about. No matter what you might sweep away, and to what position you might attain, it could always be said, 'He married a woman who used to keep a tavern.' Now, every one who is a friend to you, who knows what is before you, if you choose to try for it, should do everything that can be done to prevent such a thing ever being said of you. I am a friend to you, and I am going to prevent it."

I stood unable to say one word. Her voice, her eyes, even the manner in which she stood before me, assured me that she meant everything she said. It was almost impossible to believe that such an amiable creature could turn into such an icicle.

"I do not want you to feel worse than you can help," she said, "but it was necessary for me to speak as firmly and decidedly as I could, and now it is all settled."

I knew it was all settled. I knew it as well as if it had been settled for years. But, with my eyes still ardently fixed on her, I remembered the little flush when she came into the room.

"Tell me one thing," said I, "and I will go. If it were not for what you say about your position in life, and all that - if there had not been such a place as this inn - then could you - "

She moved away from me. "You are as great a bear as the other one!" she exclaimed, and turning she left the room by a door in the rear. But in the next moment she ran back, holding out her hand. "Good-bye!" she said.

I took her hand, but held it not a second. Then she was gone. I stood looking at the door which she had closed behind her, and then I left the house. There was no reason why I should

Frank R. Stockton

stay in that place another minute.

As I was about to mount my bicycle the boy came around the corner of the inn. Upon his face was a diabolical grin. The thought rushed into my mind that he might have been standing beneath the parlor window. Instinctively I made a movement towards him, but he did not run. I turned my eyes away from him and mounted. I could not kill a boy in the presence of a nurse-maid.

CHAPTER XVII

A FORECASTER OF HUMAN PROBABILITIES

I was about to turn in the direction of Walford, but then into my trouble-tossed mind there came the recollection that I had intended, no matter what happened, to call on the Larramies before I went home. I owed it to them, and at this moment their house seemed like a port of refuge.

The Larramies received me with wide-opened eyes and outstretched hands. They were amazed to see me before the end of my vacation, for no member of that family had ever come back from a vacation before it was over; but they showed that they were delighted to have me with them, be it sooner or later than they had expected, and I had not been in the house ten minutes before I received three separate invitations to make that house my home until school began again.

The house was even livelier than when I left it. There was a married couple visiting there, enthusiastic devotees of golf; one of Mr. Walter's college friends was with him; and, to my surprise, Miss Amy Willoughby was there again.

Genevieve received me with the greatest warmth, and I could see that her hopes of a gentleman friend revived. Little Clara demanded to be kissed as soon as she saw me, and I think

Frank R. Stockton

she now looked upon me as a permanent uncle or something of that kind. As soon as possible I was escorted by the greater part of the family to see the bear.

Miss Edith had welcomed me as if I had been an old friend. It warmed my heart to receive the frank and cordial handshake she gave me. She said very little, but there was a certain interrogation in her eyes which assured me that she had much to ask when the time came. As for me, I was in no hurry for that time to come. I did not feel like answering questions, and with as much animation as I could assume I talked to everybody as we went to see the bear.

This animal had grown very fat and super-contented, but I found that the family were in the condition of Gentleman Waife in Bulwer's novel, and were now wondering what they would do with it.

"You see," cried Percy, who was the principal showman, "the neighbors are all on pins and needles about him. Ever since the McKenna sisters spread the story that Orso was in the habit of getting under beds, there isn't a person within five miles of here who can go to bed without looking under it to see if there is a bear there. There are two houses for sale about a mile down the road, and we don't know any reason why people should want to go away except it's the bear. Nearly all the dogs around here are kept chained up for fear that Orso will get hold of them, and there is a general commotion, I can tell you. At first it was great fun, but it is getting a little tiresome now. We have been talking about shooting him, and then I shall have his bones, which I am going to set up as a skeleton, and it is my opinion that you ought to have the skin."

Several demurrers now arose, for nobody seemed to think that I would want such an ugly skin as that.

"Ugly!" cried Percy, who was evidently very anxious to pursue his study of comparative anatomy. "It's a magnificent skin. Look at that long, heavy fur. Why, if you take that skin and have it all cleaned, and combed out, and dyed some nice color, it will be fit to put into any room."

Genevieve was in favor of combing and cleaning, oiling and dyeing the hide of the bear without taking it off.

"If you would do that," she declared, "he would be a beautiful bear, and we would give him away. They would be glad to have him at Central Park."

The Larramies would not listen to my leaving that day. There were a good many people in the house, but there was room enough for me, and, when we had left the bear without solving the problem of his final disposition, there were so many things to be done and so many things to be said that it was late in the afternoon before Miss Edith found the opportunity of speaking to me for which she had been waiting so long.

"Well," said she, as we walked together away from the golf links, but not towards the house, "what have you to report?"

"Report?" I repeated, evasively.

"Yes, you promised to do that, and I always expect people to fulfil their promises to me. You came here by the way of the Holly Sprig Inn, didn't you?"

I assented. "A very roundabout way," she said. "It would have been seven miles nearer if you had come by the cross-road. But I suppose you thought you must go there first."

"That is what I thought," I answered.

"Have you been thinking about her all the time you have been away?"

"Nearly all the time."

"And actually cut off a big slice of your vacation in order to see her?"

I replied that this was precisely the state of the case.

"But, after all, you weren't successful. You need not tell me anything about that - I knew it as soon as I saw you this morning. But I will ask you to answer one thing: Is the decision final?"

I sighed - I could not help it, but she did not even smile. "Yes," I said, "the affair is settled definitely."

For a minute or so we walked on silently, and then she said: "I do not want you to think I am hard-hearted, but I must say what is in me. I congratulate you, and, at the same time, I am sorry for her."

At this amazing speech I turned suddenly towards her, and we both stopped.

"Yes," said she, standing before me with her clear eyes fixed upon my face, "you are to be congratulated. I think it is likely she is the most charming young woman you are ever likely to meet - and I know a great deal more about her than you do, for I have known her for a long time, and your acquaintance is a very short one - she has qualities you do not know anything about; she is lovely! But for all that it would be very wrong for you to marry her, and I am glad she had sense enough not to let you do it."

"Why do you say that?" I asked, a little sharply.

"Of course you don't like it," she replied, "but it is true. She may be as lovely as you think her - and I am sure she is. She may be of good family, finely educated, and a great many more things, but all that goes for nothing beside the fact that for over five years she has been the landlady of a little hotel."

"I do not care a snap for that!" I exclaimed. "I like her all the better for it. I - "

"That makes it worse," she interrupted, and as she spoke I could not but recollect that a similar remark had been made to me before. "I have not the slightest doubt that you would have been perfectly willing to settle down as the landlord of a little hotel. But if you had not - even if you had gone on in the course which father has marked out for you, and you ought to hear him talk about you - you might have become famous, rich, nobody knows what, perhaps President of a college, but still everybody would have known that your wife was the young woman who used to keep the Holly Sprig Inn, and asked the people who came there if they objected to a back room, and if they wanted tea or coffee for their breakfast. Of course Mrs. Chester thought too much of you to let you consider any such foolishness."

I made no answer to this remark. I thought the young woman was taking a great deal upon herself.

"Of course," she continued, "it would have been a great thing for Mrs. Chester, and I honor her that she stood up stiffly and did the thing she ought to do. I do not know what she said when she gave you her final answer, but whatever it was it was the finest compliment she could have paid you."

I smiled grimly. "She likened me to a bear," I said. "Do you call that a compliment?"

Edith Larramie looked at me, her eyes sparkling. "Tell me

one thing," she said. "When she spoke to you in that way weren't you trying to find out how she felt about the matter exclusive of the inn?"

I could not help smiling again as I assented.

"There!" she exclaimed. "I am beginning to have the highest respect for my abilities as a forecaster of human probabilities. It was like you to try to find out that, and it was like her to snub you. But let's walk on. Would you like me to give you some advice."

"I am afraid your advice is not worth very much," I answered, "but I will hear it."

"Well, then," she said, "I advise you to fall in love with somebody else just as soon as you can. That is the best way to get this affair out of your mind, and until you do that you won't be worth anything."

I felt that I now knew this girl so well that I could say anything to her. "Very well, then," said I; "suppose I fall in love with you?"

"That isn't a very nice speech," she said. "There is a little bit of spitefulness in it. But it doesn't mean anything, anyway. I am out of the competition, and that is the reason I can speak to you so freely. Moreover, that is the reason I know so much about the matter. I am not biassed. But you need have no trouble - there's Amy."

"Don't say Amy to me, I beg of you!" I exclaimed.

"Why not?" she persisted. "She is very pretty. She is as good as she can be. She is rich. And if she were your wife you would want her to talk more than she does, you would be so glad to listen to her. I might say more about Amy, but

I won't."

"Would it be very impolite," said I, "if I whistled?"

"I don't know," she said, "but you needn't do it. I will consider it done. Now I will speak of Bertha Putney. I was bound to mention Amy first, because she is my dear friend, but Miss Putney is a grand girl. And I do not mind telling you that she takes a great interest in you."

"How do you know that?" I asked.

"I have seen her since you were here - she lunched with us. As soon as she heard your name mentioned - and that was bound to happen, for this family has been talking about you ever since they first knew you - she began to ask questions. Of course the bear came up, and she wanted to know every blessed thing that happened. But when she found out that you got the bear at the Holly Sprig her manner changed, and she talked no more about you at the table.

"But in the afternoon she had a great deal to say to me. I did not know exactly what she was driving at, and I may have told her too much. We said a great many things - some of which I remember and some I do not - but I am sure that I never knew a woman to take more interest in a man than she takes in you. So it is my opinion that if you would stop at the Putneys' on your way home you might do a great deal to help you get rid of the trouble you are now in. It makes me feel something like a spy in a camp to talk this way, but I told you I was your friend, and I am going to be one. Spies are all right when they are loyal to their own side."

I was very glad to have such a girl on my side, but this did not seem to be a very good time to talk about the advantages of a call upon Miss Putney.

In spite of all the entreaties of the Larramie family, I persisted in my intention of going on to Walford the next morning, and, in reply to their assurances that I would find it dreadfully dull in that little village during the rest of my vacation, I told them that I should be very much occupied and should have no time to be dull. I was going seriously to work to prepare myself for my profession. For a year or two I had been deferring this important matter, waiting until I had laid by enough money to enable me to give up school-teaching and to apply myself entirely to the studies which would be necessary. All this would give me enough to do, and vacation was the time in which I ought to do it. The distractions of the school session were very much in the way of a proper contemplation of my own affairs.

"That sounds very well," said Miss Edith, when there was no one by, "but if you cannot get the Holly Sprig Inn out of your mind, I do not believe you will do very much 'proper contemplation.' Take my advice and stop at the Putneys'. It can do you no harm, and it might help to free your mind of distractions a great deal worse than those of the school."

"By filling it with other distractions, I suppose you mean," I answered. "A fickle-minded person you must think me. But it pleases me so much to have you take an interest in me that I do not resent any of your advice."

She laughed. "I like to give advice," she said, "but I must admit that I sometimes think better of a person if he does not take it. But I will say - and this is all the advice I am going to give you at present - that if you want to be successful in making love, you must change your methods. You cannot expect to step up in front of a girl and stop her short as if she were a runaway horse. A horse doesn't like that sort of thing, and a girl doesn't like it. You must take more time about it. A runaway girl doesn't hurt anybody, and, if you are active enough, you can jump in behind and take the reins and stop her gradually without hurting her feelings, and then, most likely, you can drive her for all the rest of your life."

"You ought to have that speech engraved in uncial characters on a slab of stone," said I. "Any museum would be glad to have it."

I had two reasons besides the one I gave for wishing to leave this hospitable house. In the first place, Edith Larramie troubled me. I did not like to have any one know so much about my mental interior - or to think she knew so much. I did not like to feel that I was being managed. I had a strong belief that if anybody jumped into a vehicle she was pulling he would find that she was doing her own driving and would allow no interferences. I liked her very much, but I was sure that away from her I would feel freer in mind.

The other reason for my leaving was Amy Willoughby. During my little visit to her house my acquaintance with her had grown with great rapidity. Now I seemed to know her very well, and the more I knew her the better I liked her. It may be vanity, but I think she wanted me to like her, and one reason for believing this was the fact that when she was with me - and I saw a great deal of her during the afternoon and evening I spent with the Larramies - she did not talk so much, and when she did speak she invariably said something I wanted to hear.

Remembering the remarks which had been made about her by her friend Edith, I could not but admit that she was a very fine girl, combining a great many attractive qualities, but I rebelled against every conviction I had in regard to her. I did not want to think about her admirable qualities. I did not want to believe that in time they would impress me more forcibly than they did now. I did not want people to imagine that I would come to be so impressed. If I stayed there I might almost look upon her in the light of a duty.

The family farewell the next morning was a tumultuous one. Invitations to ride up again during my vacation, to come and spend Saturdays and Sundays, were intermingled with earnest injunctions from Genevieve in regard to a correspondence which she wished to open with me for the benefit of her mind, and declarations from Percy that he would let me know all about the bear as soon as it was decided what would be the best thing to happen to him, and entreaties from little Clara that I would not go away without kissing her good-bye.

But amid the confusion Miss Edith found a chance to say a final word to me. "Don't you try," she said, as I was about to mount my bicycle, "to keep those holly sprigs in your brain until Christmas. They are awfully stickery, they will not last, and, besides, there will not be any Christmas."

"And how about New-Year's Day?" I asked.

"That is the way to talk," skid she. "Keep your mind on that and you will be all right."

As I rode along I could not forget that it would be necessary for me to pass the inn. I had made inquiries, but there were no byways which would serve my purpose. There was nothing for me to do but keep on, and on I kept. I should pass so noiselessly and so swiftly that I did not believe any one would notice me, unless, indeed, it should be the boy. I earnestly hoped that I should not see the boy.

Whether or not I was seen from the inn as I passed it I do not know. In fact, I did not know when I passed it. No shout of immature diabolism caught my ear, no scent of lemon came into my nostrils, and I saw nothing but the line of road directly in front of me.

CHAPTER XVIII

REPENTANCE AVAILS NOT

When I was positively certain that I had left the little inn far behind me, I slackened my speed, and, perceiving a spreading tree by the road-side, I dismounted and sat down in the shade. It was a hot day, and unconsciously I had been working very hard. Several persons on wheels passed along the road, and every time I saw one approaching I was afraid that it might be somebody I knew, who might stop and sit by me in the shade. I was now near enough to Walford to meet with people from that neighborhood, and I did not want to meet with any one just now. I had a great many things to think about and just then I was busy trying to make up my mind whether or not it would be well for me to stop at the Putneys'.

If I should pass without stopping, some one in the lodge would probably see me, and the family would know of my discourtesy, but, although it would have been a very simple thing to do, and a very proper thing, I did not feel sure that I wanted to stop. If Edith Larramie had never said anything about it, I think I would surely have made a morning call upon the Putneys.

After I had cooled off a little I rose to remount; I had not decided anything, but it was of no use to sit there any longer.

Glancing along the road towards Walford, I saw in the distance some one approaching on a wheel. Involuntarily I stood still and watched the on-coming cyclist, who I saw was a woman. She moved steadily and rapidly on the other side of the road. Very soon I recognized her. It was Miss Putney.

As she came nearer and nearer I was greatly impressed with her appearance. Her costume was as suitable and becoming for the occasion as if it had been an evening dress for a ball, and she wheeled better than any woman cyclist I ever saw. Her head was erect, her eyes straight before her, and her motion was rhythm of action.

With my hand on my wheel I moved a few steps towards the middle of the road. I was about to take off my cap when she turned her eyes upon me. She even moved her head a little so as to gaze upon me a few seconds longer. Her face was quiet and serene, her eyes were large, clear, and observant. In them was not one gleam of recognition. Turning them again upon the road in front of her, she sped on and away.

For some minutes I stood looking after her, utterly astonished. I do not think in all my life I had ever been cut like that. What did it mean? Could she care enough about me to resent my stopping at the Holly Sprig? Was it possible that she could have known what had been likely to happen there, and what had happened there? All this was very improbable, but in Cathay people seemed to know a great many things. Anyway, she had solved my problem for me. I need give no further thought to a stop at her father's mansion.

I mounted and rode on, but not rapidly. I was very much moved. My soul grew warm as I thought of the steady gaze of the eyes which that girl had fixed upon me. For a mile or so I moved steadily and quietly in a mood of incensed dignity. I pressed the pedals with a hard and cruel tread. I did not understand. I could scarcely believe.

Soon, however, I began to move a little faster. Somehow or other I became conscious that there was a bicycle at some distance behind me. I pushed on a little faster. I did not wish to be overtaken by anybody. Now I was sure there was a wheel behind me. I could not hear it, but I knew it was there.

Presently I became certain that my instincts had not deceived me, for I heard the quick sound of a bicycle bell. This was odd, for surely no one would ring for me to get out of the way. Then there was another tinkle, a little nearer.

Now I sped faster and faster. I heard the bell violently ringing. Then I thought, but I am not sure, that I heard a voice. I struck out with the thrust of a steam-engine, and the earth slipped backward beneath me like the water of a mill-race. I passed wagons as if they had been puffs of smoke, and people on wheels as though they were flying cinders.

In some ten minutes I slackened speed and looked back. For a long distance behind me not a bicycle was in sight. I now pursued my homeward way with a warm body and a lacerated heart. I hated this region which I had called Cathay. Its inhabitants were not barbarians, but I was suffering from their barbarities. I had come among them clean, whole, with an upright bearing. I was going away torn, bloody, and downcast.

If the last words of the lady of the Holly Sprig meant the sweet thing I thought they meant, then did they make the words which preceded them all the more bitter. The more friendly and honest the counsels of Edith Larramie had grown, the deeper they had cut into my heart. Even the more than regard with which my soul prompted me to look back to Amy Willoughby was a pain to me. My judgment would enrage me if it should try to compel me to feel as I did not want to feel.

But none of these wounds would have so pained and disturbed me had it not been for the merciless gaze which that dark-eyed girl had fixed upon me as she passed me standing in the road. And if she had gone too far and had done more than her own nature could endure, and if it were she who had been pursuing me, then the wound was more cruel and the smart deeper. If she believed me a man who would stop at the ringing of her bell, then was I ashamed of myself for having given her that impression.

CHAPTER XIX

BEAUTY, PURITY, AND PEACE

I now proposed to wheel my way in one long stretch to Walford. I took no interest in rest or in refreshment. Simply to feel that I had done with this cycle of Cathay would be to me rest, refreshment, and, perhaps, the beginning of peace.

The sun was high in the heavens, and its rays were hot, but still I kept steadily on until I saw a female figure by the road-side waving a handkerchief. I had not yet reached her, but she had stopped, was looking at me, and was waving energetically. I could not be mistaken. I turned and wheeled up in front of her. It was Mrs. Burton, the mother of the young lady who had injured her ankle on the day when I set out for my journey through Cathay.

"I am so glad to see you," she said, as she shook hands with me. "I knew you as soon as my eyes first fell upon you. You know I have often seen you on the road before we became acquainted with you. We have frequently talked about you since you were here, and we did not expect you would be coming back so soon. Mr. Burton has been hoping that he would have a chance to know you better. He is very fond of school-masters. He was an intimate friend of Godfrey Chester, who had the school at Walford some years before you came - when the boys and girls used to go to school together - and of the man who came afterwards. He was a little too elderly, perhaps, but Mr. Burton liked him too, and now he hopes that he is going to know you. But excuse me for keeping you standing so long in the road. You must come in. We shall have dinner in ten minutes. I was just coming home from a neighbor's when I caught sight of you."

I declined with earnestness. Mr. Burton might be a very agreeable man, but I wanted to make no new acquaintances then. I must keep on to Walford.

But the good lady would listen to no refusals of her hospitality. I was just in time. I must need a mid-day rest and something to eat. She was very sorry that Mr. Burton was not at home. He nearly always was at home, but to-day he had gone to Waterton. But if I would be contented to take dinner with her daughter and herself, they would be delighted to have me do so. She made a motion to open the gate for me, but I opened it for her, and we both went in. The daughter met us at the top of the garden walk. She came towards me as a cool summer breeze comes upon a hot and dusty world. There was, no flush upon her face, but her eyes and lips told me that she was glad to see me before she spoke a word or placed her soft, white hand in mine. At the first touch of that hand I felt glad that Mrs. Burton had stopped me in the road. Here was peace.

That dinner was the most soothing meal of which I had ever partaken. I did the carving, my companions did the questioning, and nearly all the conversation was about myself. Ordinarily I would not have liked this, but every word which was said by these two fair ladies - for the sweetness of the mother was merely more seasoned than that of the daughter - was so filled with friendly interest that it gratified me to make my answers.

They seemed to have heard a great deal about me during my

wanderings through Cathay. They knew, of course, that I had stopped with the Putneys, for I had told them that, but they had also heard that I had spent a night at the Holly Sprig, and had afterwards stayed with the Larramies. But of anything which had happened which in the slightest degree had jarred upon my feelings they did not appear to have heard the slightest mention.

I might have supposed that only good and happy news thought it worth while to stop at that abode of peace. As I looked upon the serene and tender countenance of Mrs. Burton I wondered how a cloud rising from want of sympathy with early peas ever could have settled over this little family circle; but it was the man who had caused the cloud. I knew it. It is so often the man.

When we had finished dinner and had gone out to sit in the cool shadows of the piazza, I let my gaze rest as often as I might upon the fair face of that young girl. Several times her eyes met mine, but their lids never drooped, their tender light did not brighten. I felt that she was so truly glad to see me that her pleasure in the meeting was not affected one way or the other by the slight incident of my looking at her.

If ever a countenance told of innocence, purity, and truth, her countenance told of them. I believe that if she had thought it pleased me to look at her, it would have pleased her to know that it gave me pleasure.

As I talked with her and looked at her, and as I looked at her mother and talked with her, it was impressed upon me that if there is one thing in this world which is better than all else, it is peace, that peace which comprises so many forms of happiness and deep content. That the thoughts which came to me could come to a heart so lacerated, so torn, so full of pain as mine had been that morning, seemed wonderful, and yet they came.

Frank R. Stockton

Once or twice I tried to banish these thoughts. It seemed disrespectful to myself to entertain them so soon after other thoughts which I now wished to banish utterly. I am not a hero of romance. I am only a plain human being, and such is the constitution of my nature that the more troubled and disturbed is my soul, the more welcome is purity, truth, and peace.

But, after all, my feelings were not quite natural, and the change in them was too sudden. It was the consequence of too violent a reaction, but, such as it was, it was complete. I would not be hasty. I would not be deficient in self-respect. But if at that moment I had known that this was the time to declare what I wished to have, I would unhesitatingly have asked for beauty, purity, and peace.

A maid came out upon the piazza who wanted something. Mrs. Burton half rose, but her daughter forestalled her. "I will go," said she. "Excuse me one minute."

If my face expressed the sentiment, "Oh, that the mother had gone!" I did not intend that it should do so. Mrs. Burton then began to talk about her daughter.

"She is like her father," she said, "in so many ways. For one thing, she is very fond of school-masters. I do not know exactly why this should be, but her teachers always seem to be her friends. In fact, she is to marry a school-master - that is, an assistant professor at Yale. He is in Europe now, but we expect him back early in the fall."

A short time after this, when the daughter had returned and I rose to go, the young girl put her soft, white hand into mine exactly as she had done when I arrived, and the light in her eyes showed me, just as it had showed me before, the pleasure she had taken in my visit. But the mother's farewell was different from her greeting. I could see in her kind air a certain considerate sympathy which was not there before. She had been very prompt to tell me of her daughter's engagement.

That young angel of peace and truth would not have deemed it necessary to say a word about the matter, even to a young man who was a school-master, and between whom and her family a mutual interest was rapidly growing. But with the mother it was otherwise. She had seen the shadows pass away from my countenance as I sat and talked upon that cool piazza, my eyes bent upon her daughter. Mothers know.

CHAPTER XX

BACK FROM CATHAY

The next morning, being again settled in my rooms in Walford, I went to call upon the Doctor and his daughter. The Doctor was not at home, but his daughter was glad to see me.

"And how do you like your cycle of Cathay?" she asked.

"I do not like it at all," I answered. "It has taken me upon a dreary round. I am going to change it for another as soon as I have an opportunity."

"Then it has not been a wheel of fortune to you?" she remarked. "And as for that country which you figuratively called Cathay, did you find that pleasant?"

"In some ways, yes, but in others not. You see, I came back before my vacation was over, and I do not care to go there any more."

She now wanted me to tell her where I had really been and what had happened to me, and I gave her a sketch of my adventures. Of course I could not enter deeply into particulars, for that would make too long a story, but I told her where I had stopped, and my accounts of the bear and the horse were deeply interesting.

"It seems to me," she said, when I had finished, "that if things had been a little different, you might have had an extremely pleasant tour. For instance, if Mr. Godfrey Chester had been living, I think you would have liked him very much, and it is probable that you would have been glad to stay at his inn for several days. It is a beautiful country thereabout."

"Did you know him?" I asked.

"Oh yes," she said; "he was my teacher during part of my school-days here. And then there is Mr. Burton; father is very fond of him. He is a man of great intelligence. It was unfortunate that you did not see more of him."

"Perhaps you know Mr. Putney?" I said.

"No," she answered. "I have heard a great deal about him. He seems to be a stiff sort of a man. But as to Mr. Larramie, everybody likes him. He is a great favorite throughout the county, and his son Walter is a rising young man. I am glad you made the acquaintance of the Larramies."

"So am I," I said, "very glad indeed. And, by-the-way, do you know a young man named Willoughby? I never heard his first name, but he lives at Waterton."

"Oh, the Willoughbys of Waterton," she said. "I have heard a great deal about them. Father used to know the old gentleman. He was a great collector of rare books, but he is dead now. If you had met him you would have found him a man of your own tastes."

When I was going away she stopped me for a moment. "I forgot to ask you," she said; "did you take any of those capsules I gave you when you were starting off on your cycle?"

"Yes," said I, "I took some of them." But I could not well explain the capricious way in which I had endeavored to guard against the germs of malaria, and to call my own attention to the threatening germs of erratic fancy.

"Then you do not think they did you any good?" she said.

"I am not sure," I replied. "I cannot say anything about that. But of one thing I am certain, and that is, that if any germs of any kind entered my system, it is perfectly free from them now."

"I am glad to hear that," she said.

It was about a week after this that I received a letter from Percy Larramie. "I thought you would like to know about the bear," he wrote. "Somebody must have forgotten to feed him, and he broke his chain and got away. He went straight over to the Holly Sprig Inn, and I expect he did that because the inn was the last place he had seen his master. I did not know bears cared so much for masters. He didn't stay long at the inn, but he stayed long enough to bite a boy. Then he went into the woods.

"As soon as we heard of it we all set off on a bear-hunt. It was jolly fun, although I did not so much as catch a sight of him. Father shot him at a three-hundred-foot range. It was a Winchester rifle with a thirty-two cartridge. It was a beautiful shot, Walter said, and I wish I had made it.

"We took his skin off and tore it only in two or three places, which can be mended. Would you like to have the skin, and do you care particularly about the head? If you don't, I would like to have it, because without it the skeleton will not be perfect."

I wrote to Percy that I did not desire so much as a single hair of the beast. I did not tell him so, but I despised the bears of Cathay.

It was just before the Christmas holidays when I finally made up my mind that of all the women in the world the Doctor's daughter was the one for me, and when I told her so she did not try to conceal that this was also her own opinion. I had seen the most charming qualities in other women, and my somewhat rapid and enthusiastic study of them had so familiarized me with them that I was enabled readily to perceive their existence in others. I found them all in the Doctor's daughter.

Her father was very well pleased when he heard of our compact. It was plain that he had been waiting to hear of it. When he furthermore heard that I had decided to abandon all thought of the law, and to study medicine instead, his satisfaction was complete. He arranged everything with affectionate prudence. I should read with him, beginning immediately, even before I gave up my school. I should attend the necessary medical courses, and we need be in no hurry to marry. We were both young, and when I was ready to become his assistant it would be time enough for him to give me his daughter.

We were sitting together in the Doctor's library and had been looking over some of the papers of the Walford Literary Society, of which we were both officers, when I said, looking at her signature: "By-the-way, I wish you would tell me one thing. What does the initial 'E.' stand for in your name? I never knew any one to use it."

"No," she said; "I do not like it. It was given to me by my mother's sister, who was a romantic young lady. It is Europa.

Frank R. Stockton

And I only hope," she added, quickly, "that you may have fifty years of it."

*   *   *   *   *

Three years of the fifty have now passed, and each one of the young women I met in Cathay has married. The first one to go off was Edith Larramie. She married the college friend of her brother who was at the house when I visited them. When I met her in Walford shortly after I heard of her engagement, she took me aside in her old way and told me she wanted me always to look upon her as my friend, no matter how circumstances might change with her or me.

"You do not know how much of a friend I was to you," she said, "and it is not at all necessary you should know. But I will say that when I saw you getting into such a dreadful snarl in our part of the country, I determined, if there were no other way to save you, I would marry you myself! But I did not do it, and you ought to be very glad of it, for you would have found that a little of me, now and then, would be a great deal more to your taste than to have me always."

Mrs. Chester married the man who had courted her before she fell in love with her school-master. It appeared that the fact of her having been the landlady of the Holly Sprig made no difference in his case. He was too rich to have any prospects which might be interfered with.

Amy Willoughby married Walter Larramie. That was a thing which might well have been expected. I was very glad to hear it, for I shall never fail to be interested in the Larramies.

About a year ago there was a grand wedding at the Putney city mansion. The daughter of the family was married to an Italian gentleman with a title. I read of the affair in the newspapers, and having heard, in addition, a great many details of the match from the gossips of Walford, I supposed myself to be fully informed in regard to this grand alliance, and was therefore very much surprised to receive, personally, an announcement of the marriage upon a very large and stiff card, on which were given, in full, the various titles and dignities of the noble bridegroom. I did not believe Mr. Putney had sent me this card, nor that his wife had done so; certainly the Count did not send it. But no matter how it came to me, I was very sure I owed it to the determination, on the part of some one, that by no mischance should I fail to know exactly what had happened. I heard recently that the noble lady and her husband expect to spend the summer at her father's country-house, and some people believe that they intend to make it their permanent home.

The Doctor strongly advises that Europa and I should go before long and settle in the Cathay region. He thinks that it will be a most excellent field for me to begin my labors in, and he knows many families there who would doubtless give me their practice.

Choose from Thousands of 1stWorldLibrary Classics By

A. M. Barnard
Ada Leverson
Adolphus William Ward
Aesop
Agatha Christie
Alexander Aaronsohn
Alexander Kielland
Alexandre Dumas
Alfred Gatty
Alfred Ollivant
Alice Duer Miller
Alice Turner Curtis
Alice Dunbar
Allen Chapman
Alleyne Ireland
Ambrose Bierce
Amelia E. Barr
Amory H. Bradford
Andrew Lang
Andrew McFarland Davis
Andy Adams
Angela Brazil
Anna Alice Chapin
Anna Sewell
Annie Besant
Annie Hamilton Donnell
Annie Payson Call
Annie Roe Carr
Annonaymous
Anton Chekhov
Archibald Lee Fletcher
Arnold Bennett
Arthur C. Benson
Arthur Conan Doyle
Arthur M. Winfield
Arthur Ransome
Arthur Schnitzler
Arthur Train
Atticus
B.H. Baden-Powell
B. M. Bower
B. C. Chatterjee
Baroness Emmuska Orczy
Baroness Orczy
Basil King
Bayard Taylor
Ben Macomber
Bertha Muzzy Bower
Bjornstjerne Bjornson

Booth Tarkington
Boyd Cable
Bram Stoker
C. Collodi
C. E. Orr
C. M. Ingleby
Carolyn Wells
Catherine Parr Traill
Charles A. Eastman
Charles Amory Beach
Charles Dickens
Charles Dudley Warner
Charles Farrar Browne
Charles Ives
Charles Kingsley
Charles Klein
Charles Hanson Towne
Charles Lathrop Pack
Charles Romyn Dake
Charles Whibley
Charles Willing Beale
Charlotte M. Braeme
Charlotte M. Yonge
Charlotte Perkins Stetson
Clair W. Hayes
Clarence Day Jr.
Clarence E. Mulford
Clemence Housman
Confucius
Coningsby Dawson
Cornelis DeWitt Wilcox
Cyril Burleigh
D. H. Lawrence
Daniel Defoe
David Garnett
Dinah Craik
Don Carlos Janes
Donald Keyhoe
Dorothy Kilner
Dougan Clark
Douglas Fairbanks
E. Nesbit
E. P. Roe
E. Phillips Oppenheim
E. S. Brooks
Earl Barnes
Edgar Rice Burroughs
Edith Van Dyne
Edith Wharton

Edward Everett Hale
Edward J. O'Biren
Edward S. Ellis
Edwin L. Arnold
Eleanor Atkins
Eleanor Hallowell Abbott
Eliot Gregory
Elizabeth Gaskell
Elizabeth McCracken
Elizabeth Von Arnim
Ellem Key
Emerson Hough
Emilie F. Carlen
Emily Bronte
Emily Dickinson
Enid Bagnold
Enilor Macartney Lane
Erasmus W. Jones
Ernie Howard Pie
Ethel May Dell
Ethel Turner
Ethel Watts Mumford
Eugene Sue
Eugenie Foa
Eugene Wood
Eustace Hale Ball
Evelyn Everett-green
Everard Cotes
F. H. Cheley
F. J. Cross
F. Marion Crawford
Fannie E. Newberry
Federick Austin Ogg
Ferdinand Ossendowski
Fergus Hume
Florence A. Kilpatrick
Fremont B. Deering
Francis Bacon
Francis Darwin
Frances Hodgson Burnett
Frances Parkinson Keyes
Frank Gee Patchin
Frank Harris
Frank Jewett Mather
Frank L. Packard
Frank V. Webster
Frederic Stewart Isham
Frederick Trevor Hill
Frederick Winslow Taylor

Friedrich Kerst
Friedrich Nietzsche
Fyodor Dostoyevsky
G.A. Henty
G.K. Chesterton
Gabrielle E. Jackson
Garrett P. Serviss
Gaston Leroux
George A. Warren
George Ade
Geroge Bernard Shaw
George Cary Eggleston
George Durston
George Ebers
George Eliot
George Gissing
George MacDonald
George Meredith
George Orwell
George Sylvester Viereck
George Tucker
George W. Cable
George Wharton James
Gertrude Atherton
Gordon Casserly
Grace E. King
Grace Gallatin
Grace Greenwood
Grant Allen
Guillermo A. Sherwell
Gulielma Zollinger
Gustav Flaubert
H. A. Cody
H. B. Irving
H.C. Bailey
H. G. Wells
H. H. Munro
H. Irving Hancock
H. R. Naylor
H. Rider Haggard
H. W. C. Davis
Haldeman Julius
Hall Caine
Hamilton Wright Mabie
Hans Christian Andersen
Harold Avery
Harold McGrath
Harriet Beecher Stowe
Harry Castlemon
Harry Coghill
Harry Houidini

Hayden Carruth
Helent Hunt Jackson
Helen Nicolay
Hendrik Conscience
Hendy David Thoreau
Henri Barbusse
Henrik Ibsen
Henry Adams
Henry Ford
Henry Frost
Henry James
Henry Jones Ford
Henry Seton Merriman
Henry W Longfellow
Herbert A. Giles
Herbert Carter
Herbert N. Casson
Herman Hesse
Hildegard G. Frey
Homer
Honore De Balzac
Horace B. Day
Horace Walpole
Horatio Alger Jr.
Howard Pyle
Howard R. Garis
Hugh Lofting
Hugh Walpole
Humphry Ward
Ian Maclaren
Inez Haynes Gillmore
Irving Bacheller
Isabel Cecilia Williams
Isabel Hornibrook
Israel Abrahams
Ivan Turgenev
J.G.Austin
J. Henri Fabre
J. M. Barrie
J. M. Walsh
J. Macdonald Oxley
J. R. Miller
J. S. Fletcher
J. S. Knowles
J. Storer Clouston
J. W. Duffield
Jack London
Jacob Abbott
James Allen
James Andrews
James Baldwin

James Branch Cabell
James DeMille
James Joyce
James Lane Allen
James Lane Allen
James Oliver Curwood
James Oppenheim
James Otis
James R. Driscoll
Jane Abbott
Jane Austen
Jane L. Stewart
Janet Aldridge
Jens Peter Jacobsen
Jerome K. Jerome
Jessie Graham Flower
John Buchan
John Burroughs
John Cournos
John F. Kennedy
John Gay
John Glasworthy
John Habberton
John Joy Bell
John Kendrick Bangs
John Milton
John Philip Sousa
John Taintor Foote
Jonas Lauritz Idemil Lie
Jonathan Swift
Joseph A. Altsheler
Joseph Carey
Joseph Conrad
Joseph E. Badger Jr
Joseph Hergesheimer
Joseph Jacobs
Jules Vernes
Julian Hawthrone
Julie A Lippmann
Justin Huntly McCarthy
Kakuzo Okakura
Karle Wilson Baker
Kate Chopin
Kenneth Grahame
Kenneth McGaffey
Kate Langley Bosher
Kate Langley Bosher
Katherine Cecil Thurston
Katherine Stokes
L. A. Abbot
L. T. Meade

L. Frank Baum
Latta Griswold
Laura Dent Crane
Laura Lee Hope
Laurence Housman
Lawrence Beasley
Leo Tolstoy
Leonid Andreyev
Lewis Carroll
Lewis Sperry Chafer
Lilian Bell
Lloyd Osbourne
Louis Hughes
Louis Joseph Vance
Louis Tracy
Louisa May Alcott
Lucy Fitch Perkins
Lucy Maud Montgomery
Luther Benson
Lydia Miller Middleton
Lyndon Orr
M. Corvus
M. H. Adams
Margaret E. Sangster
Margret Howth
Margaret Vandercook
Margaret W. Hungerford
Margret Penrose
Maria Edgeworth
Maria Thompson Daviess
Mariano Azuela
Marion Polk Angellotti
Mark Overton
Mark Twain
Mary Austin
Mary Catherine Crowley
Mary Cole
Mary Hastings Bradley
Mary Roberts Rinehart
Mary Rowlandson
M. Wollstonecraft Shelley
Maud Lindsay
Max Beerbohm
Myra Kelly
Nathaniel Hawthrone
Nicolo Machiavelli
O. F. Walton
Oscar Wilde

Owen Johnson
P.G. Wodehouse
Paul and Mabel Thorne
Paul G. Tomlinson
Paul Severing
Percy Brebner
Percy Keese Fitzhugh
Peter B. Kyne
Plato
Quincy Allen
R. Derby Holmes
R. L. Stevenson
R. S. Ball
Rabindranath Tagore
Rahul Alvares
Ralph Bonehill
Ralph Henry Barbour
Ralph Victor
Ralph Waldo Emmerson
Rene Descartes
Ray Cummings
Rex Beach
Rex E. Beach
Richard Harding Davis
Richard Jefferies
Richard Le Gallienne
Robert Barr
Robert Frost
Robert Gordon Anderson
Robert L. Drake
Robert Lansing
Robert Lynd
Robert Michael Ballantyne
Robert W. Chambers
Rosa Nouchette Carey
Rudyard Kipling
Saint Augustine
Samuel B. Allison
Samuel Hopkins Adams
Sarah Bernhardt
Sarah C. Hallowell
Selma Lagerlof
Sherwood Anderson
Sigmund Freud
Standish O'Grady
Stanley Weyman
Stella Benson
Stella M. Francis

Stephen Crane
Stewart Edward White
Stijn Streuvels
Swami Abhedananda
Swami Parmananda
T. S. Ackland
T. S. Arthur
The Princess Der Ling
Thomas A. Janvier
Thomas A Kempis
Thomas Anderton
Thomas Bailey Aldrich
Thomas Bulfinch
Thomas De Quincey
Thomas Dixon
Thomas H. Huxley
Thomas Hardy
Thomas More
Thornton W. Burgess
U. S. Grant
Upton Sinclair
Valentine Williams
Various Authors
Vaughan Kester
Victor Appleton
Victor G. Durham
Victoria Cross
Virginia Woolf
Wadsworth Camp
Walter Camp
Walter Scott
Washington Irving
Wilbur Lawton
Wilkie Collins
Willa Cather
Willard F. Baker
William Dean Howells
William le Queux
W. Makepeace Thackeray
William W. Walter
William Shakespeare
Winston Churchill
Yei Theodora Ozaki
Yogi Ramacharaka
Young E. Allison
Zane Grey

www.ingramcontent.com/pod-product-compliance
Lightning Source LLC
Chambersburg PA
CBHW020125180626
46810CB00004B/1410